A Haunted Murder

A Novella in the Maui Mystery Series

§

Kay Hadashi

A Haunted Murder

A Haunted Murder
A Novella in the Maui Mystery Series.
Kay Hadashi.
Copyright 2019. © All Rights Reserved.

ISBN: 9781098937515

This story is a work of fiction. Character names and attributes, places, and situations are completely fictitious, products of imagination, and should not be considered real. Information related to current events should be considered common knowledge and can be easily found in real life. Historical situations, stories, and characters are completely fictitious and should not be considered reflective of actual historical events.

Cover art by author. Original cover image from pixabay.com

3

A Haunted Murder

Table of Contents

Prologue

Kaimanakeali'i sat on his wicker throne, two boys fanning him with bundles of sacred ti leaves. Finished with a meal of poi and fish, he set the wooden bowl aside, feeling quite satisfied with himself. He was still young enough that he craved a stick of sugar cane as a sweet dessert, but as Molokai's newest ali'i, he was determined to play the part of chief to the hilt. As it was, he was still enjoying his first week of marriage to the island's most beautiful young woman, Luanapua. That meant dessert could still be enjoyed, something even sweeter than the cane that grew around their village.

"Where is my Pua?" he asked, *pua* being one of the many Hawaiian words for flowers. "Fixing a haku garland of bridal flowers for her head?"

"She is taking a rest," an old man said. Keanukakai was one of the young chief's advisors, an old family friend, a hanai uncle. But for fate and circumstances, he had never been tapped as chief of the island, always serving someone else. "Unfortunately, there are no more flowers from the wedding."

"No more ho'okupu of flowers? Where have our gifts gone?"

The old advisor stepped closer to young Kaimanakeali'i to explain. "Yes, you see, each time you take Luanapua to the betrothal hut, there are fewer flowers to be had. She must rest occasionally."

"Rest? Have I married a weak girl?"

"It's the way of women. You must treat them gently. Otherwise, they become quite cross with their husbands."

"I am the ali'i of this island! If someone is to become cross, it is me who has that privilege! We were wed before the god Hina, and the union has been blessed. Now, bring me my wife."

The wrinkled old Keanukakai leaned even closer. "Maybe another girl from the village? You've always favored Kahula, the dancer. Maybe she could tell you a story with her hips and arms one last time while you wait for your Luanapua to recover?"

"But what about my Pua?" Kaimana asked quietly.

"She would never know. It would be a blessing for her to have the day off from your rather bold attention."

"This meeting with Kahula would take place in the betrothal hut?"

"Of course not. You could use my humble little hut anytime you wish."

"And you'll arrange this meeting?" Kaimana asked.

"Immediately! As soon as I can find the lovely Kahula." Keanukakai sent away the fan wavers to find bowls of water for Kaimana to bathe. "You understand it is best to keep these things secret, yes? Especially from our wives."

"You've done the same thing?"

"Many times. The fact you don't know about the clandestine endeavors of married men shows how well a secret can be kept on an island such as ours."

Two hours later, after a meal of poi, fish, and sweet potatoes had been served, and sugar cane chewed,

Kaimana moved in for the kill. It was an easy task with Kahula, as she had been his first woman. Not that he had known many others. In fact, the only reason she had not been selected to be his wife was because of all the men she had known. Just as they were pulling a heavy tapa cloth over them for privacy, someone approached, their footsteps across the rocky ground announcing their arrival.

An empty wooden serving bowl was flung and skipped off the young aliʻi's back. "Kaimanakealiʻi! You dog!"

Kaimana eased with what he was doing with Kahula but didn't quit altogether. "My Pua! What are you doing here?"

"Me? Better to ask you!" Luanapua aimed an accusatory finger at her rival Kahula as though it were a woman's best weapon. "And with her!"

Kahula tried to squirm from beneath Kaimana's large body. "Maybe I should go, my lover."

"Your lover!" screamed Luanapua. She threw another bowl that bounced off Kaimana's head. Bits of leftover fish flew in every direction.

When Kaimana seemed reluctant to end the moment, Luanapua pulled the tapa cloth from off the lovers. Still in the midst of their tryst, Luanapua shrieked.

"It's okay, my Pua. The wise old Keanukakai said this sort of thing is done all the time," Kaimana begged, reaching for the tapa cloth.

"That foolish old kanaka? Of course he thinks that! He's father to half the children on this island! And I hate to break it to you at this moment, but you're not Kahula's only lover. If you don't believe me, just ask every wife on Molokai! Including Keanukakai's wife!" She grabbed hold of the thick barkcloth blanket and pulled with all her might. "Stop what you're doing and get back to our hut this instant!"

"But my Pua…" Kaimana complained.

"Leave that woman alone before I call for the rage of the gods to plague you forever more!"

Kaimana did his best to walk with dignity from the humble little hut back to his own. Once he was gone, Luanapua and Kahula locked eyes.

"And you!" Luanapua yelled at her childhood friend. "Stay away from my husband or you'll find yourself dead when you wake in the morning!"

After Luanapua stormed off, the two old men hiding in the bushes watched as Kahula dressed slowly.

"Keanukakai, you old fool, you've really made a mess of things this time."

"Quiet, Kaleo. This is going perfectly according to my plan."

"Which is?"

"Get that young fool out of the way and put the rightful ali'i on the throne."

"And who might that be?" Kaleo asked.

"For three generations, who has been the rightful owner of the feathered cloak and headdress of the ali'i of Molokai?" Keanukakai asked. He was watching Kahula continue to dress, with the fastest heartbeat he'd suffered in ages.

10

"How could I have forgotten? You haven't moaned over the fact of not being on the throne for at least a day. But how will you get rid of our young aliʻi?"

"Kill him."

"Kill an aliʻi?" Kaleo asked. Suddenly, nerves crept into his voice. "He is too well protected for something like that. It might be best to banish him and his Luanapua from the village."

"Yes, good idea. I know exactly how to do it, too. But to where? Another island?"

"To the City of Refuge near Kawela on the coast," Kaleo offered.

"That place is too good for him. Those villagers can fish from their canoes, and have all the fresh water they need to grow food. No, I want him to suffer thirst and hunger like no islander has ever known."

"So, once you are wearing the cloak of the aliʻi, you make a new village, one only for him, and in the driest, most terrible place on this island. A refuge for the doomed."

"Yes, good idea, Kaleo. And I could send that Luanapua with him. But how would we keep them there? That Luanapua is wise beyond her years. She'd find a way for them to escape their misery."

"What if you put them there, and Kanela the kahunaʻanaʻana kept them there with one of her magic spells?"

"Kanela, the village hula teacher? Rumor has it she is the mother to Kahula. That's how that little tramp got her name. They say even the daughter has some magical powers," Keanukakai said.

"All the more reason why Kanela would want to help you." Kaleo raised up to get a better view of Kahula. "It also explains why the daughter is so popular, if she has magical powers of her own."

"She has some of her mother's magic," Keanukakai said.

"Kahula has...her mother's magic...wait. You mean you and Kanela and Kahula?"

"Not all at the same time, you old fool. But trust me, there is good reason why Kahula is so popular with the men on the island, and has few friends among the women."

"One of the reasons you've lived such a long life, my old chum," Kaleo said, patting his friend on the back.

Keanukakai watched the young woman finish fixing her long hair and replace her haku head garland of flowers. "One of the many reasons."

"Maybe you shouldn't have brought her into this little drama you've started with our new ali'i and his young wife. You'll have too many women madder than hungry sharks, and when they sense blood in the water, I'm afraid it's going to be yours."

"We can keep the City of Refuge at Kawela as a second choice if the cursed village for the doomed doesn't work."

"Keanukakai, make it your first choice. You can even use some of Kahula's magic to trap them there. Nobody would ever guess it came from her, and they would never be able to find a cure for it. Kaimana and Luanapua would be trapped in Kawela for all of eternity." Kaleo could see his argument was falling on deaf ears. "If you had your way, by whose hand will Kaimana's demise as ali'i come?"

"By the only person that can come close enough to him: his jealous wife. But first, we must deal with another," Keanukakai said, watching Kahula leave the hut.

"Her?"

"Her."

"How?"

"Get rid of her."

"You mean…" Kaleo asked with wide eyes.

"Kill her. But only once we're done using her as bait one last time."

"But we all suffer if she makes the long voyage to Heaven," Kaleo complained. "I do like her magical ways."

"Her sister is nearly old enough and twice as beautiful. With any luck, some goddess blood may have spilled into her soul, and brought some magic with it."

"So, what's the plan?" Kaleo asked.

"We just need to convince Kahula to perform a moment of magic to trap Kaimanakeali'i and Luanapua at their own cursed village, and then kill her. Once all three are gone, I take over as ali'i of Molokai. That's the plan, plain and simple."

Now that Kahula was gone, they went to Keanukakai's hut and tossed the tapa cloth to one side before sitting. Both the hut and the decorated barkcloth had witnessed many trysts spanning many years, and that day wasn't the first time it had felt the soft curves of Kahula's body beneath it.

"And how do you propose it's done?" Kaleo asked.

"Like I said, use Kanela's magic. That part I'll leave to her, promising some vague reward for her effort."

"And to get rid of the witness?" Kaleo asked.

"You mean Kahula? By making sure she wakes to find herself dead one morning," Keanukakai said. "Just like Luanapua promised her moments ago. I'm sure we weren't the only ones in the village to have heard her make that promise."

"I'm confused. Don't we want Kai...someone else to perish?"

"One at a time, old friend. One at a time."

Chapter One

It was Halloween, and the few kids in costumes at the Maui airport sat with empty Trick or Treat buckets while they waited with their parents for flights.

As a treat for her kids, and a break from her busy schedule as surgeon, small business owner, and county mayor, Melanie was taking the family and nanny to Molokai for the weekend. As it was, with a storm brewing out to sea, she wasn't sure if there would be much Trick or Treating in the small town where they would stay on Molokai, one of the islands she was responsible for as mayor. If the storm cancelled flights and shut down airports on Sunday, they would be stranded on Molokai, barely a dozen miles across the Lahaina Channel from Maui, but a world away from home and work. But the plane tickets were paid for, the house rented for the weekend, and promises of Halloween fun and games made to the children.

"Do I look like a dinosaur, Momma?" Thérèse, Melanie's six-year-old daughter, asked. She was wearing a one-piece purple and green outfit that went from head to toe, and had a droopy tail in back.

"You sure do, Sweetie. Hana did a great job making that for you."

"Yes, well, it could fit a little better," Hana, the nanny, said, picking at the fit. It looked like a baggy scuba outfit, purple with green spots.

"She'll grow into it," Melanie said. "Not sure how she'll get past TSA wearing that, though."

"What's Brother supposed to be again?" the girl asked, examining her two-year-old brother.

"Tom Sawyer."

"What's a thumb slayer?"

"No, Tom Sawyer. He's a famous boy in a book. In a few more years, you can read about him. You're sure you're not too hot wearing that?" Melanie asked.

"I okay. Can I ask those people for Trick or Treaties?"

"No treats until this evening. Anyway, we have to eat dinner first."

"I can eat candy tonight?" the girl asked.

"Two pieces."

The girl spun around in a circle. "Yay!"

Melanie quickly revised her promise. "Two small pieces. And three tomorrow, just like we already talked about."

"Brother too?"

"Yes, your brother, too," Melanie said with a sigh.

With nothing else better to do than sit and wait at their gate, Melanie got out her phone to make a call. Her first grader daughter was busy watching other travelers go to and from terminals, while her two-year-old son reduced a piece of fruit leather to pulp. The number she dialed was one she had been calling often recently, for a number of reasons: her personal lawyer.

"David, what's the news on the ownership of the Napili Winds resort? Did you ever find an actual personal name? Or is it corporate owned?"

"It's corporate, but somebody owns the corporation, and that's the sticking point. Those corporate owners have shadows and mirrors everywhere. I can't determine if it's owned by someone in Hawaii or someone on the mainland. I do know it's not owned by the Japanese or Chinese. These types of ownership things are well guarded, Melanie. Why are you so interested in it, anyway?"

"I know it's not locally owned. If it was, they'd make a big deal out of it in marketing. For some reason I've always had the idea the owner was New York based. Even back when I worked there as a teenager in housekeeping."

"That doesn't explain why you're so interested in knowing who the owner is," David Melendez said. Not only was he her lawyer but also a cousin, and a partner in one of LA's most powerful law firms. She tried hard not to bother him with minor personal matters, but when a recent murder investigation turned against her, she brought him in, reconnecting after many years. She also rarely enjoyed the benefits of being a President's daughter, living a quiet life on Maui. David, on the other hand, tapped into his uncle's good name by writing his own ticket to the best colleges and law school, and quickly became partner in the Melendez firm. But the time had come for Melanie to use her pull, and her father's name.

"I told you, the resort is planning on putting up new condo and guest towers, along with swimming pools and tennis courts, using that large lawn."

"That's called growth, Melanie. Tourism to Hawaii, and Maui specifically, is at an all-time high in popularity."

"Tell me about it. My house is right across the road from where they want to build," she said. "I really don't want more growth right there, and Maui certainly doesn't need more hotel rooms. Between Kihei and Ka'anapali, resorts barely hit eighty percent occupancy even during the high seasons, and barely fifty percent in shoulder seasons. Building new towers would be good for employment figures for the year they're under construction, but the resulting employment once they're open would be low paying jobs and those employees would have to come from central Maui, a long drive away. Once again, most of the profits would go off island into mainland banks. From what I've been hearing from constituents, Mauians would rather not have to deal with increased traffic in West Maui, and would rather have the open space to enjoy."

"And you're worried they'll block the view of the sunset?"

She ground a knuckle into her eye socket in an effort to stop the tic that was making her eyelid twitch. "It might be more personal than that."

"What are your plans when I do find the owner?" he asked.

"I don't know. Try and stop them somehow. Buy the place if I have to."

"Buy the lawn? What would you do with a lawn? You'd spend all your time mowing."

"Buy the whole doggone resort, if it comes to that."

"You have the money and you certainly aren't using it for anything else. But I just don't see you as an hotelier."

"Ha! Me either. I'm not much good at running a sporting goods store or restaurant, either. In fact, I'm thinking of letting someone else manage those completely and go back to work at the hospital full-time."

"You're one of the Pacific Rim's best surgeons. I can't understand why you don't. Is there anything else? I have a meeting in a few minutes. Did you get the latest divorce requests from Josh yet?"

"They were delivered this morning. I haven't looked, though."

"Melanie, just sign the papers, give him some cash, and be done with it."

"That...he's not getting cash, and he's not getting the kids. All he's getting from me is a black eye."

"Maybe leave the athletic stuff for after the divorce is final," David said.

"If I ever see him again, he better be wearing a cup in his whitie-tighties. If he can find one small enough to fit."

David laughed. "Too much information, Melanie. Got to go. I'll send you what I learn in a couple of days."

Their plane still hadn't arrived, so she made another call, this time to a man who worked at her father's other business, a security and intelligence firm.

"Bruce. Ever find Ozzy?"

"Your old friend? Still working on it. Why are you at the airport? Running away from home?" he asked.

Bruce had a way of digging op dirt on people the FBI and federal intelligence organizations were unable to find.

"Just for the weekend. But no word on Ozzy? And he's definitely not an old friend."

"Last verifiable sighting was on Oahu, along the North Shore."

"When?"

"Three weeks ago. He was using an alias and pretending to be a big wave surf instructor."

Melanie laughed, even though just thinking about her old nemesis made her anxious. "I've seen him on a board. If surfing had a bunny slope, he'd have a hard time with it."

"Well, we're still monitoring your GPS signals, your kids, and both of your nannies. If he gets within a hundred meters of any of you, we'll send a text to your phone."

"Let me know if he shows up on Maui," Melanie said, before ending that call and watched as a plane rolled to a stop at the terminal gate. Hana had taken Chance to play in a quiet corner of the waiting area.

"Momma, was that Daddy?" Thérèse asked.

"It was your Uncle David in California. He says hello. Do you remember him?"

She nodded. "Wears fancy kind clothes."

"Sure does. Speaking of nice clothes, I wish you would've worn your new muumuu for the flight. You don't need to wear your dinosaur costume until this evening."

Thérèse was obviously struggling to sit still. "But not allowed to play in my muumuu. No can get it dirty. Anyhow, this is Helloweed and I'm a dinosaur."

"It's pronounced Halloween. And you're being a very good girl sitting still. You and Chance are going to have a lot of fun this weekend, and both of you can get as dirty as you want when we go to the beach tomorrow. But we have to be careful at a beach we don't know, okay?"

"Other kids gonna be there?" Thérèse asked.

"Probably a few. Maybe we can find some this evening for Trick or Treating. But you have to be a good girl. This isn't home. We're only visitors here."

Thérèse's face twisted thoughtfully, turning into a wince. "Well, no garbentees about being a good girl."

"Garbentee? Oh, guarantee. No, I suppose not after you've had candy." Melanie sighed. "Just do your best…" She leaned over to whisper in the girl's ear. "…and try not to use your magic too often, okay?"

"I try, Momma. Momma, is Daddy going to be at Mol'kai?"

"I hope…I don't think so. Molokai is a long way from Wyoming."

"Daddy not here no more?"

"No, not any more. He went home to be with his mother, remember?"

"When's he gonna come back?"

Watching passengers stream through the gate from the interisland flight that had just landed, Melanie scooted closer to her daughter. "Sweetie, we've talked about that a bunch of times. I don't think he's coming home anymore. It's just you and Chance and me from now on."

"And Hana and Georgie?"

"Yes, and your serendipitously interchangeable nannies. But I'm not sure how much longer they're staying with us. Georgie is thinking about moving back to Honolulu and Hana might go home to Japan. We've talked about that, also. It might be time to find a new nanny, and the same one all the time, instead of switching back and forth between two of them."

Thérèse was in a full-blown pout by now, meaning tears weren't far away. From what Melanie could tell from their family conversations was that the girl was as upset about losing her nannies as she was over missing her father. To save the moment, Hana returned with children's books she'd found at the gift shop.

Just as Thérèse was beginning to read to her brother from a book about dinosaurs, their flight was called. It took longer to load and unload than it took to make the hop from one island to the other.

That weekend trip to their neighboring island of Molokai was a simple get-away, requiring only one bag each. Once Thérèse and Chance had their Ariel and Moana knapsacks adjusted on their backs, and Melanie and Hana had the rest of their suitcases, they went to the arrivals curb to look for the ride Melanie had arranged.

"Me and Brother been here before, Momma?" Thérèse asked.

Even though Chance was well beyond two years old, he still wasn't speaking much, mostly just names of people and simple greetings. He did, however, have some sort of peculiar ability to 'communicate' with Thérèse without actually speaking, what the girl called 'thinking' to her.

"Nope. Whenever I come here, it's by myself for a day."

"Yeah, you're mayor of Mol'kai, huh?"

"For a few more weeks."

"Are there kids on Mol'kai?"

"Sure are."

The girl began to hop. "Can we find some?"

"Of course. We'll find some kids for you and Chance to go Trick or Treating with. And tomorrow, we can go to a park."

"There's a park?" Hana asked. "How far do we have to walk to take the kids there?"

"Just a few blocks from the house. The place we're staying in is new, but I remember the area. My mother and I stayed in the same neighborhood once when I was a kid. The park is small but good enough to run off some energy."

"We'll use up most of our energy just walking everywhere this weekend," the nanny complained.

"You been here with your momma?" the girl asked, once Melanie finished her call to their driver.

"Yes, and we had lots of fun. We went exploring all over the place. Tomorrow, we can go exploring in the little town."

"Why didn't we get a rental car and a room in a hotel?" Hana asked. It turned out that Hana enjoyed the resort lifestyle as much as the other nanny did, and tended to whine when they didn't stay at something with at least three stars on their weekend junkets.

"Our House has a car available. We just need a ride to get there. And after seeing the pictures of the house, it's just as nice as any resort," Melanie said. "It'll be fun."

"Is there a pool with cabana boys, or a spa with masseurs?" Hana asked, a subtle whine slipping in already.

"It has large suites, air-conditioning, and a complete kitchen that we can use as much as we want."

Hana sulked. "Oh, good. More home cooking, even on a weekend vacation."

"Sploring for what, Momma?" Thérèse asked.

That question put Melanie in a bind, and she wanted the distraction of the car to keep from answering. Nearly forty years before, she and her mother had come to Molokai for a wedding and spent their spare time on ghost hunting adventures, checking out gloomy closed resorts and haunted ancient lava fields with secret caves containing skeletons. As it turned out, the trip became family legend for finding more than what they bargained for.

"Different places. I remember a nice beach. Maybe we can go there if we have time."

"Georgie says there's ghosts on Mol'kai," the girl said. "Lots of them. Nightfarters, too."

"They're called nightmarchers, and no, we're not going to look for them."

"For why not?"

"Because they're very dangerous and bring a lot of trouble." Saving her from any further explanation, their ride arrived. The van had Hale Pakele stenciled on the side, with colorful orchids as a trademark.

"Ready for an exciting time at Hale Pakele?" the young Hawaiian man asked enthusiastically, once everybody was in his van.

"Sure are," Melanie said.

"Are there kids there?" Thérèse asked.

"Only you guys. You seem familiar."

"My momma is mayor of Maui. Mol'kai, too!" Thérèse announced.

"Oh, yes, Mayor Kato, chief of our county. Sorry, I didn't connect the name."

"That's okay. I won't be mayor for much longer."

"What about the election next week? Are you voting for that Nakatani fellow? From reading in the newspaper, the two of you know each other rather well."

"I only know him as a police detective working for Maui Police Department. Otherwise, the people of Maui County will speak with their ballots."

"You didn't want to run for a second term?" the driver asked.

"I barely wanted this term. The only reason I got it was because the mayor was thrown in prison, and I got stuck with the job because I came in second place in the last election."

"Well, you've done a nice job."

"Thanks. Not so sure if I've done anything for the people of Molokai, though."

"That's the thing. We like having this place as a refuge from the rest of the world. You've left us alone to our own business and haven't meddled in Molokai's affairs."

"Maybe I should've done the same with everybody else."

She watched the scenery as the van got to the edge of town. A large house with a thatched roof loomed in the distance, surrounded by palms and lush vegetation, something she remembered seeing in the travel brochure. She had selected the Hale Pakele because of the Hawaiian motif, something she was hoping would be fun and educational for the others. While it was privately owned, the owners lived in Honolulu, and rented it out for special occasions, like weddings and meetings. The modern luxury house was in the style of older Polynesian architecture, with a steeply pitched thatched roof, dark wood siding, and long, louvered windows hidden beneath deep eaves. Several smaller buildings surrounded the main home, connected by open-air corridors. Lava rock walls made for small garden areas, with bamboo, banana plants, and palms providing protection and shade. A mockup of a watery taro patch was out front, surrounded by a circular driveway that passed beneath a large portico at the front entrance to the home. Large clusters of ti plants waved in the breeze at each side of the main entrance. It looked more like a village-style resort than a private home.

What was peculiar was that it was very near to the bed and breakfast Melanie and her mother had stayed at decades before, just on the edge of town. She recognized the neighborhood from seeing the park and a small convenience store nearby.

"Is there a little B&B near here named Auntie Sandra's, or something like that?"

"Auntie Sandra! All the old timers on Molokai knew her. You know Auntie?"

"I met her as a kid."

"Oh, well, that place is no more. The Hale Pakele was built right on top of her old place. Some say the new place is still haunted by the same ancient ghosts that were at Auntie's."

"I wish you wouldn't have said that," Melanie muttered, just as they were going through the main gate in the middle of a high rock wall. Not only had she met one or two of those ghosts in the past, there was a hideous secret about the area surrounding the estate. She also didn't want to plant any ideas in Thérèse's mind about ghosts, nor in the superstitious mind of Hana. Just like many Japanese, she was tuned into the supernatural as much as Melanie was, even though they both tried their best not to be.

"Is that your Halloween costume?" the driver asked Thérèse while getting bags from the van.

The girl spun on her toes. "I'm a dino! Brother is Tom Sour. Are there Trick'r Treaters around here?"

"If you go out, be careful. It's a full moon tonight," he said. "Well, I should get going. Something about this place gives me the creeps."

When Melanie tried offering a tip, he seemed to be in a hurry to leave. "You'll be back Sunday afternoon to pick us up?"

"If you stay here that long."

Chapter Two

Once the van left, Melanie was dragged to the small taro garden in the middle of the circular driveway by Thérèse. Hana followed, bringing Chance with her. Water gurgled out of a lava grotto like a natural spring feeding a pond, and Melanie wondered how much engineering must've gone into the pump system, and what the electric bill was each month to run it. Not only was taro growing in the wet patch, but sweet potatoes, yams, and greens around the edges. In the pond were fish, a type Melanie couldn't recognize. They seemed energetic and acted as though they expected to be fed. The scene must've looked magical to Thérèse, who looked intently into the dark grotto where the water was coming from.

"That where the ghosties live?"

"I don't think so. Very pretty garden, though."

"You seen them like this before?"

"A few. This is a Hawaiian garden, how they grew their food in the past. I think some still do."

"Are there ghosties in Hawaiian gardens?" Thérèse asked.

"I don't know. I hope there aren't any watching us." Melanie watched as Thérèse edged around behind her to hide. "They can see you back there, too."

"Don't want the ghosties watching me."

"I think the ghosts only come out at night."

"What's the big surprise, Melanie?" Hana asked, keeping Chance restrained from going into the pond.

"This!" Melanie said, sweeping her hand through the air.

Hana made a point of looking around. "This what?"

"It's supposed to look like a Hawaiian village. It'll be fun, and we have the whole place to ourselves, with the household staff dedicated to us as though we're royalty. This is why we're staying here, so we can see this type of house and garden."

"Oh, good," Hana said drolly. "A field trip with home cooking."

"We won't have to do any cooking."

"I'd rather have fruity drinks with little umbrellas served by cabana boys and daily massages," Hana hissed, pulling Chance away from the pond again.

There was the low rumble of thunder coming from the sea, catching all of their attention. A few raindrops came with a second rumble.

"And now it rains," Hana said.

"Momma, we still can go treating, right?"

"Definitely, even if we have to borrow umbrellas." Melanie saw one of the house staff wearing a tidy muumuu-style uniform waiting under the portico. "It's starting to rain, so maybe we should go inside and find our rooms? I've heard they have another bigger garden in back of the house that we can explore later."

"Ghosties in it?"

"That's why we have to explore. Go get your brother and bring him in the house before the two of you get wet."

The main building was mostly a large living area arranged like a casual living room decorated with wicker furniture, woven floor mats, and with several seating areas around the sides. A large kitchen was hidden toward the back. All of the sleeping and privacy areas were in surrounding cabanas. With the way it was arranged, it gave the home a village feel, with the communal area in the middle where everyone could gather. It was aptly named 'The Oahu Room', meaning 'the gathering place'.

The four of them were shown to 'The Molokai Suite', a large cabana of two bedrooms, two beds each, and a spacious bathroom, separate from but connected to the main building by a covered outdoor walkway. The Polynesian motif was everywhere, with lava rock accents, wicker furniture, and woven mat flooring. Hana immediately switched on the A/C to combat the growing humidity now that the rain was coming.

Since they would be there for a long weekend, Melanie got their things unpacked. Thérèse was dedicated to wearing her dino costume, reluctant to give up on Trick or Treating that evening, even if heavy rain was starting. Listening to pleas from her daughter to find other kids, it became time for Thérèse to take a nap just as Chance was waking from his. Melanie made a game of playing airplane with Chance, holding him over her while on her back on the bed. When her phone rang, she started a new game of driving a car using a pillow as a steering wheel. He made the engine noises to go along with the game.

"Mayor Kato? This is Chief Hernandez. Do you have a moment?"

"Not really. I told you twice this week that I would be going out of town on the weekend, and that Vice Mayor Trinh Park would field anything related to City Hall business. You need to call her."

"Actually, this is a police business call unrelated to you being mayor."

"If there has been a serious crime, put detectives on it or whatever you normally do. Otherwise, if there is a citizen complaint, just tell them there's nothing I can do about crime or police matters in one weekend. Whatever it is will have to wait until Monday."

"It pertains directly to you."

"What about me?"

"It's about your restaurant. Nobody has called you?" he asked.

"What about the restaurant? Get to the point, Chief. Did someone skip out without paying the bill again?"

"Worse than that. Your manager called to report a burglary."

Melanie sat up. "Burglary?"

"When the manager got there to open the place, she found the door broken in."

Melanie rubbed a knuckle into the tic that was starting in one eye. "What was stolen?"

"Apparently, everything."

"We keep the cash locked in a safe while the store is closed, so the damage can't be too bad. Hopefully, they didn't take some of the better cookware. That stuff is expensive."

"Well, it was the cookware, along with dishes, silver, tables, chairs, linens. They even cleared out the coolers, then took the coolers and stoves."

"What? That's everything!"

"That's not the end of the list. They removed the carpeting, took the cash register, even the light fixtures. Apparently, the place is cleared out of everything that can be removed, from top to bottom."

"Those…" Melanie almost swore but modified it for Chance's ears. "Somebody could open a new restaurant with all that."

"That's what Detective Nakatani is thinking. He's looking into all new restaurants on the island, to see if any of it shows up there."

"Nakatani is investigating? You can't put someone else on it?"

"I know how the two of you feel about each other, but he was up for the next assignment. What's that noise? Are you driving somewhere?" he asked.

"No, I'm playing with my son. Not that it makes much difference now, but is there a way of locking the door to the restaurant? I don't want people living in there."

"Not from the sounds of it. Want me to find someone to board it up?"

"I'll take care of it, thanks." Melanie ended that call and phoned a friend that owned a spa next door to Melanie's restaurant. Surely, she would've noticed something. "Lai, do you know anything about my restaurant being broken into today?"

"What? Nothing. I started getting cancellations because of the weather, so I closed up early and came home. What happened?"

Melanie explained what she knew about the burglary. "Is Duane there?"

Her old Air Force Search and Rescue buddy came onto the call. He was the general manager of Maui's largest hardware store. "Sorry about your place, Melanie. Do you need the door boarded up?"

"Can you? I hate to send you out in this weather."

"We went out in worse weather than this back in our Air Force days. I have some news, though. I'm in line for a promotion."

"Promotion? That's great! But I thought you were already at the top of the business ladder for the store?"

"It would be corporate. If I get it, Lai, the kids, and I would move to the mainland."

"Oh, the mainland." That was something she had never considered, that two of her best friends would leave the island. "When will you know?"

"Not for a few weeks. There are several applicants, so I doubt I'd get it. Hey, I should get started on boarding up your place. We'll talk later."

She looked at her phone after the call, already feeling a little heartbroken over the news. "Yeah, talk later."

Thérèse romped in, re-energized from her nap. Going back out to find a staff member with the kids, Melanie was surprised at how large the house was walking through it.

"We're very happy to meet you and your family, Mayor Kato. My name is Luana, and I'll be in charge of the house for the weekend. If you need anything at all, please don't hesitate to let me know." The professional young Polynesian woman had a spray of freckles across her nose and cheeks, and wore little jewelry but for a puka shell necklace. In spite of her pleasant demeanor, she looked tense about something. "Unfortunately the weather might not be good."

"It's already begun to rain, and I saw dark clouds in the distance from the plane," Melanie said. "The airline gate agent said something about flights being delayed throughout the islands, but it just seemed a little windy to me."

"It's come up rather suddenly," the young woman said. "Do you have sightseeing plans for the weekend?"

"Trick or Treating with the kids this evening, if this rain stops for a while. Maybe you can tell us where to go? My daughter seems more interested in finding other kids than in getting candy."

"She's very sweet. If the weather isn't bad tomorrow, and you're not busy with anything else, I can draw a map to a few places on the island for you to visit."

To assist with cross-flow ventilation, windows and sliding doors were open throughout the house, and the entrance to the back garden was through an open wall with large sliders that could be closed in windy weather. When the rain began to pound down ever harder, the staff went to close a few of the doors to keep the wind out.

Once Luana excused herself to check on dinner preparation, Melanie and her mini entourage toured each part of the main house, inspecting old paintings from the days of the whaling industry, long spears, clubs, and daggers used by Hawaiian warriors in battles over island rule. There were even a few lava stones that had been removed from their native positions outside to be used as décor in the house. They had images of people, fish, and birds etched into them as petroglyphs, making them museum pieces.

"Fancy stuff, huh, Momma?"

"Sure is."

"Can we put a big rock in our house?"

"Our house is already a little crowded even without rocks in it."

The last place they went was into the main living room. By then, it was dark outside and the rain was harder than ever.

"Looks like we're out of luck with going Trick or Treating tonight, Tay."

"Even with 'brellas?"

"We'd get soaked, and I doubt anybody else will be out in this weather. We'll find some way of having fun here at the house, I promise. First, I smell dinner. Let's go see what we're having."

A large woven mat made from the slender leaves of hala plants was already set up on the floor, along with several wooden bowls, in preparation for an authentic Hawaiian meal that would be served for dinner.

"Dinner will be ready in a few more minutes," Luana came to tell them, and hurried off again.

With no one else around, it seemed lonely but for two things: along one wall was a display of an ali'i's red and yellow feather cloak, something only Hawaiian royalty would've worn in the past. On a stand in front of it rested a large feathered helmet, obviously ceremonial. Deep red feather kahili standards stood at attention on either side of the cloak. At the front of the display were a few implements of battle: a pair of shark tooth-edged wooden clubs, pointed spears, and a battle mace weighted with a lava rock at one end. One spear in particular looked like a ceremonial piece that was probably used by the chief of the island, the same one who would've worn the feathered outfit. Everything looked weather beaten as though they were antiques that belonged in a museum.

Adjacent to that display was a woman's thick skirt made from bunches of ti leaves. A few simple pieces of jewelry were there that the ali'i's wife would've worn, shell or kukui nut necklaces, bracelets, and anklets. A freshly woven ti leaf haku head garland rested on a small table. Whoever owned the grand home went to a great deal of trouble to have knock-off garments and implements made to look authentic.

"Lookit, Momma. Who wore all those feathers?"

"Those were for the chief of the island. You'll learn more about them in your Hawaiian classes at school."

"Do you have feather clothes? You're chief of Maui, right?"

"Tay, have you ever seen me wear feathers?"

"Maybe you could get some mayor feathers?"

"I think we'll leave the feathers on the birds where they belong."

Chance was disinterested in the displays, so Hana started a game of hide and seek in the vast room. Thérèse wasn't done with her inspection tour of the ancient garments. She positioned herself in front of the implements of battle.

"What's all that stuff for?"

"That's what warriors used in ancient Hawaii for battle." Melanie had seen similar things in museums, heavy clubs used to break bones and crack skulls, jagged shark tooth swords to slash and gash bodies, pointed spears to impale chests, and long braided ropes for tripping the enemy. "Really terrible things, huh?"

"Used them in big fights?"

"That's right."

"You used those when you were a soldier, Momma?"

"No, I had something else."

"Were you the soldier chief with feathers on your clothes?" the girl asked.

"I wore Kevlar instead of feathers. You've seen pictures of me back then."

"Yeah, you were young then."

Melanie looked down at her daughter. "Yeah, thanks."

Thérèse was now intently looking at a large club on a stand. "What's that big thing for?"

Melanie knew exactly what it was, and how it was used, but didn't want to tell her daughter the details. "It's a club, just like the others."

"Club for what?"

"For finishing a fight."

"How for was it used?" the girl asked after more inspection.

"Okay, I'll tell you but it's super-duper scary. You're sure you want to know?"

Thérèse took a step back and edged closed to her mother. "Guess so."

"Well, at the end of the day of battle, the warriors would go out to the battlefield one last time looking for survivors. They didn't have hospitals back then, and the warriors that were injured real bad would die sooner or later. So the other ones would use that club to help them along."

"Help 'em along where?" the girl asked, setting her eyes on the club again.

"To Heaven."

The girl winced. "That a magic club?"

"No, Sweetie. They'd knock the injured guys over the head until they were dead. That way they could go to Heaven sooner and not have to suffer. It was their way of showing mercy for the injured." With the clothing and the swords on display the way they were, Melanie decided another lesson was in order, if only to warn Thérèse off from getting too curious about the weapons. "In some ways you were right, that these things were magical. Even though those battle weapons were terrible in killing, the Hawaiians believed they had a sort of spirit to them, that they were almost alive. Those things were considered sacred. You know what that word means, right?"

Thérèse looked up at her mother with big eyes. "Sorta like they had God in them?"

"That's exactly right," Melanie said, pulling her daughter from her hiding spot behind her. "So, you better not play with those or there will be big trouble, okay?"

"I don't want any trouble with the Hawaiian battle guys," the girl said, clutching to her mother's clothes.

Luana, the staff in charge of the house, came to them.

"I just got a text message from the emergency storm center that the storm is still growing."

Melanie rubbed her forehead. "I guess I picked the wrong weekend to go out of town. Any idea if Maui is getting much of this storm?"

"I'm sure eventually it will. What part of the island do you live on?"

"Ka'anapali. Maybe it won't be so bad there."

"Your home should be okay," Luana said, making it sound reassuring.

A man came to them with a new weather report. "The other side of the island is really catching right now. The brunt of the storm should be here any time. Hopefully, the power won't go out. I sure would like to give City Hall a piece of my mind about our light service going on and off every time the wind blows the wrong way."

Luana shifted her weight from one foot to the other, then back again. Using it like punctuation, she cleared her throat.

"Kaimana, this is Mayor Kato. She and her family are staying with us for the weekend. Since she's mayor of Maui, Lanai, and Molokai, maybe you'd like to give her a piece of your mind in person?"

"That's okay," Melanie said politely. "Message delivered. I get frustrated by it also. I was just thinking I should try and get home."

As if on cue, the lights flickered in the house, bringing a nervous laugh to each of them.

"You're certainly welcome to stay here at the house until the storm blows over," the man said. He re-introduced himself as Kaimana, an old-fashioned Hawaiian name. His voice was deep and booming, a reflection of his size. He was well dressed but casually. "It is a pleasure to meet someone of your stature. You've come a long way to visit us here on Molokai. I wish to extend every courtesy and blessing to you and your family."

"Thank you very much," Melanie said, and introduced her daughter. With the formal greeting, she wondered if he was a part of the family that owned the home.

"For as long as you're here, consider Hale Pakele your home." He looked down at Thérèse and grinned broadly. "It'll be wonderful having keiki here."

"Hello, Sir. I'm Thérèse. This is my Mommy, my brother Chance, and our nanny, Hana. Hana wants a massage."

Hana's face flashed red and she excused herself to go back to the room for something. With nothing else to do once Kaimana and Luana had left them, Melanie took the kids back to their suite to change clothes and get some rest before dinner.

"That guy's really big, huh, Momma?"

"Sure was."

"Was he a warrior?"

"I don't think he was old enough. Those battles happened a super long time ago."

"Did you fight in those battles?" Thérèse asked. Her legs had to work twice as fast to keep up with Melanie's long stride.

"No, even I'm not old enough to have been in ancient Hawaiian battles."

"Maybe he's a chief?"

"Maybe," Melanie said, letting them into their room. "We'll ask him later at dinner."

Dinner was what Melanie had requested, Hawaiian and all vegetarian. Poi, potatoes, yams, and various fruits and vegetables were served in large wooden bowls. Luana and Kaimana joined Melanie and the others on their hala mat, but had fish with their meals.

The storm finally got to their part of the island, with wind driving rain sideways. It wasn't expected to be a hurricane, and would hopefully blow over during the night, allowing them to explore the island the next day.

"Some weather," Melanie said to break the silence at the meal. "I'm always surprised thatched roofs hold up in weather like this and don't leak."

"We're hopeful the roof stays on. This house was just recently built and hasn't been through any storms yet."

That wasn't reassuring to Melanie. The last thing she wanted was to find another place to spend the night if trouble came. As it was, she was having a hard time keeping her mind off the news about her restaurant back home. "I see."

"You should be fine tonight, if you stay in those smaller rooms. Those are quite sturdy," Luana said. "It's this main building that could be troublesome tonight. Once dinner is finished, it really would be best for all of your to remain in your suite until morning."

Melanie felt bad for Thérèse. Not only was she not going out Trick or Treating that evening, she would be stuck in the room with little to do. She also felt bad for herself and Hana, that they'd have to put up with the girl's whining. Melanie was already thinking of a way to sneak the kids out once the household staff had retired for the night.

Sitting in the spacious room made the place feel lonely for some reason, even though Thérèse carried on a game of twenty questions with Kaimana. Once he seemed to have suffered enough of her, he set his attention on Hana, the kids' nanny.

"We have a visitor from a place far from here. What is the name of your land?"

"I'm from Japan," Hana said.

Hana had gotten over most of her natural shyness while living with Melanie's family, but seemed intimidated by the large man. Or attracted to him, Melanie wasn't sure when she saw the young woman blush slightly. Then she noticed Kaimana smiling a little too broadly. Maybe it had something to do with Thérèse mentioning the massage Hana wanted.

"Another island nation! Welcome to Molokai. Your visit brightens our tropical skies."

Luana cleared her throat, causing Kaimana to glance in her direction. "It is evening, Kaimana. The clouds hide the dark skies above us."

His smile sagged slightly, but he went right back to putting his attention on Hana. "You'll be staying with us for a while?"

"Just for the weekend. I'm here with Melanie…Mayor Kato and the kids. The island seems quite nice, from what I've seen so far."

Kaimana's face brightened again. "Too bad there is so much rain. That will keep you indoors. Please let me know if there is anything I can do to make your visit more pleasurable on this lovely island evening."

Luana cleared her throat again, this time more sharply. "A storm is growing, Kaimana."

He barely paid attention. Instead, he said, "If the weather has cleared by morning, I'd like to show you our taro patches. We grow all our own food here." He passed the bowl of cooked fish to her. "These are from our pond. I noticed earlier that you were inspecting it. These are the very best fish anywhere on this island."

Luana almost barked when she cleared her throat this time. "Kaimana, our visitors aren't interested in the fish or the taro patch. I'm sure they'd like to finish their meals and get some rest after their long journey."

Once the small group was finished with their dinner, Melanie and her kids went to the living room to lounge. There was a clatter from the direction of the kitchen, maybe a bowl crashing to the floor, followed by argumentative words. Thérèse went on another inspection tour of the warrior outfits and weapons, while Melanie played a game of hide and seek with Chance. When there was a second crash and more words were exchanged, Hana looked embarrassed and excused herself.

Eventually, Thérèse returned to play in the game of hide and seek.

"Momma, that big guy likes Hana, huh?"

"Seemed like it."

"Does she like him?"

"Maybe."

There was another crash, the loudest yet, followed only by Luana's voice.

"Why is that lady so mad at him?"

"Oh, I think she's jealous." Melanie leaned close to Thérèse to share a secret. "I think they're married, and Hana got in the middle of it."

"Luana's mad at him like you're mad at Daddy?"

"Yep." Melanie sat on one of the long couches, tired of the game. She got Thérèse and sat her down next to her. "Except I'm even madder at Daddy than she is at Kaimana. Do you know why?"

The girl winced. "It's very complicated big people stuff."

"Who told you that?"

"Georgie," the girl said. Georgie was the other young woman that would fill in as nanny occasionally.

"Well, she's right. It is very complicated and I don't understand some of it myself. And I'm the one right in the middle of it."

"Was Daddy a bad boy?"

"Sure was."

"Georgie said Daddy talked to other girls besides you. He even made friends with them, and that's why you're mad at him. But you always tell me to make friends with people. Why so mad about Daddy making friends?"

"Well, he made special friends with one or two. Not like your friends at school, but more like special friends with me when he still lived with us."

"Oh. Big people can just gotta have one special friend at a time?" the girl asked.

Melanie stroked the hair from Thérèse's face. "Yep, or everybody gets mad at everybody else and there's a big mess. And when they get married, it's even more important. Does any of this make sense?"

"Sorta not really. Momma, are you and Daddy gonna be special friends again?"

"Nope."

"Gonna make special friends with other guys?"

"Oh, I doubt it. I think I've had all the special friends I'm supposed to have. But someday, you and Chance will find special people to share your lives with."

"And Hana and Georgie, too?"

"I hope so. But I'll tell you a secret. I think they both already have found someone, at least for a while."

"They gonna get married with a white dress and bunches of flowers?"

"Maybe not yet but someday." Even though the storm was officially raging outside, with palm fronds thrashing about in the wind, tree branches banging against the walls, Chance had fallen asleep on the couch through the noise.

Luana came out from the back of the house where the kitchen was, and forced a smile.

"The rest of the staff have gone home because of the storm. Kaimana and I are going to our room. If you need anything, just help yourself to the kitchen. But please let me remind you to remain in your suite tonight."

"The two of you live here?" Melanie asked.

"Yes, in the private residence behind the kitchen. Please don't go out in the storm or open any of the doors. I know it's a little scary to be cooped up like this, but you should be safe in your suite tonight."

"I'm sure we'll be fine," Melanie said, not entirely believing it. She already had plans to get their bags packed, just in case. She took the kids back to their suite, Luana following along to check their room.

"If things get desperate, there is a place to go for more protection." Luana pressed another smile. "But it really is best if you remain here in your room and keep the door locked tonight. Don't worry if you hear noise. Everything will be fine in the morning."

Melanie closed the door so she could talk with Luana privately. "I'm sorry if we've come at the wrong time."

"Oh, you mean the words I had with my husband earlier? Forget it. We do that occasionally. I'm afraid I'm a rather jealous wife. The problem with tonight is that it is the akua moon. That always puts us a little more on edge than usual. This storm isn't helping matters."

Melanie had her own troubles with the akua moon, from only a few years before while carrying Thérèse, but she wasn't going to bring it up right then. Instead, she wished Luana a quiet night and closed the door.

Chapter Three

It was too early to go to bed when Melanie finally had the chance to stretch out on her bed. The way the sleeping arrangements worked out was that Thérèse would have a sleepover with Hana in one room, and Chance would stay with Melanie. Even at home, he spent most nights sleeping with her. As soon as Melanie began to read a book, Chance noticed and tried climbing up onto the bed. Getting a lift from her, he snuggled in at her side.

"Momma," he whispered.

"Hello, buddy. Did you like your dinner?" she asked slowly.

Instead of answering, he reached for her book. She let him have it.

"Are you ever going to talk to me?"

He played with the pages like any small child would, watching them as they flipped one way or the other.

"I'm glad you and Sister think to each other, but I'd really like it if you talked to me, too."

Tired of feeling ignored, she took the book and set it aside. She positioned herself to look straight into his eyes.

"I'm your momma. You need to talk to me, or think to me, or something. I need you to do more than just hold my hand and wiggle around in my bed at night."

He grabbed a handful of her hair and gave it a yank.

"I was thinking of something more fun than hair pulling."

He yawned, showing off a need to have his teeth brushed.

"I really am kinda fun. Just ask your sister. She has fun with me. I bet you would also, if you'd just talk to me."

After a yawn, one of Chance's fingers got close to his mouth, which she gently pulled away.

"Okay, maybe not tonight, but someday pretty soon, right?"

Unable to win the battle with his finger sucking, she came up with a different idea.

"You know, I bet we could find some ice cream in the kitchen. Or maybe share a peanut butter sandwich?"

The boy's face seemed to brighten at her offer. He slid down from the bed and aimed for the door. She followed after him.

"Oh, sure. You understand ice cream, but forget about talking to me."

He reached up to take her hand and led her off in the direction of the kitchen. Most of the lights were off in the grand house, and just as they were passing through the large living room, the last of them flickered once and went out altogether.

Chance stopped dead in his tracks, and Melanie figured it was because of the dim light. There was just enough ambient light to illuminate their way through the sparsely furnished room. Here and there were stone bowls with small flames, burning kukui nuts and the oil they make. Along with the flames were thick smoke and an acrid odor. Someone had planned ahead by lighting the simple lamps, anticipating the electricity going out.

"We'll have to find some candles for our room if the lights stay off."

When she tugged at his hand to continue walking to the kitchen, Chance still didn't budge. His gaze was set on one place, directly on the displays of clothing. When he took a step back, she got worried.

"What is it?" she asked, looking across the dark room. That's when she saw what he was concerned about. Going across, they got to the displays of Hawaiian clothing and battle implements. As Chance edged around behind her to hide, Melanie got a chill.

Nothing was on its rack, the clothing, the weapons, the feather kahili, the feather cloak, even the fresh ti leaf head garland and skirt. All that remained were several bowls with flames flickering and pungent smoke rising, casting an eerie glow on the nearby walls.

"Maybe Luana and Kaimana put everything away because of the storm?" she muttered, trying to make sense of things. "She said something about a place that offered more protection. Maybe they really are antiques and they put them away for safe keeping."

Melanie was finally able to pry Chance loose from his spot on the floor with another promise of a treat. Sitting in the dark kitchen, they shared a bowl of chopped fruit and milk. When there was the sound of footsteps, Melanie hoped it was Luana coming with an update on the power outage, that maybe Kaimana was working on getting a generator started. Instead, it was Thérèse and Hana, also looking for a treat.

Thérèse quickly connived a way of getting scoops of ice cream with her and Chance's syrupy fruit, making Melanie wonder how much vigorous playtime would be needed before they fell asleep that night.

"Luana didn't come by?" Hana asked, sipping from a glass. She'd popped the cork on a bottle from the pantry.

"I haven't seen either one of them. Or heard them, for whatever that's worth."

There was a sudden blast of wind that made the building shudder.

"Didn't she say something about a safe place to go if the building started coming apart?" Another hard gust of wind slammed the building. "The wind is getting strong."

"She mentioned an underground storeroom. Maybe we should find it and take some water and food with us." She looked at Thérèse, now finished with her second dessert of the evening. "What about you, little girl? You want to play hide and seek from the storm?"

"Pretty scary stuff out there."

"Sure is. Maybe you and Chance should go with Hana and pack a few things in a bag. I'm going to get water and food, and find that room. Meet you back in the living room in a few minutes."

"Playing a big game, huh, Momma?"

"Not so much of a game. This is pretty important. Make sure you stay with Hana and do whatever she tells you."

The girl winced. "No trickering tonight, huh?"

"Sorry. This storm is becoming tricky enough. Even if we used an umbrella outside, we'd get soaked. Maybe we'll try tomorrow. But it might be time for you to take off your dino costume and put on regular clothes."

Melanie filled a bag with bottles of water and snack foods from the kitchen, along with candles and a set of matches, before going in search for the basement. While she did that, she used her phone to search for a cellular signal, but found nothing.

The living room looked gloomier than ever as she looked through closets for trap doors. A steady breeze was blowing through, threatening the flickering kukui oil lamps. By the time Hana and the kids returned, Melanie still hadn't found doorways that might lead downstairs. Worse than that, Hana and the kids were wet as though they had been outside in the rain.

"We need to find that safe room," Hana said. "The roof over the walkway has blown away and the roof on this part of the house was bouncing up and down all over the place. What's it called? The Oahu Room? Some gathering place."

Melanie did her best to keep panic from her voice. "Your idea of staying at a resort is sounding better all the time."

"Unfortunately, I think it's too late for that."

Checking for a cellular signal one last time, there was nothing. Making matters worse was the fact her battery was almost dead. "This isn't good. I can't find Luana or Kaimana. She said something about their living quarters being at the back of the kitchen, but the only door at the rear was to the outside. And I'm not going on a wild goose chase in the rain looking for them."

"Nobody else is around?" Hana asked.

"It looks like we're on our own for the rest of the night." Melanie pulled aside a heavy woven hala mat, exposing simple wooden floorboards but no trap doors. "We need to find that basement door."

"Does the door have to be in the floor?"

"Well, no, but I've checked everywhere else for doors. There's nothing. The only doors are to the outside. The room Luana mentioned must be a root cellar."

Thérèse winced. "Really gotta go under the floor?"

"Going into a basement is safer than staying up here."

"What about back there?" Thérèse asked, pointing a finger toward the wall behind where the displays had been.

Melanie hadn't noticed that wall earlier and went to it. Pulling away woven mats that covered the wall, she found a hidden doorway. When she saw the touchpad for a combination with the numbers arranged like on a phone, she glared at it.

"This must be a panic room the family had built into the house. It's got to be what Luana meant as a room that offered more protection." Tapping in a random number, a tiny red light came on but the door didn't open. When there was a heavy gust of wind and a loud crash outside from something bashing into a nearby wall, she looked at her family. They weren't holding up any better than she was right then. Hana was wringing her hands, Chance sucked on a finger, and Thérèse clutched at a toy.

"Momma, can we go to our room now?"

"Hana, can you go check our suite?"

Hana returned a moment later, rain-soaked all over again. "The roof is gone and the walls didn't look so good either. I noticed the other cabanas were pretty beat up also. There are palm fronds everywhere. I thought Luana said something about those rooms being sturdier than this building?"

"Both of them said a lot of things. It sounded good at the time, but they aren't making a whole lot of sense right now." Melanie paced a lap in the large room, checking doors, looking for a place that might be safest for them. Having only flickering oil lamps for light didn't help her nerves. Finally, she went back to the hidden door with the touchpad lock, and tried numbers at random.

"It's okay, Momma."

"No, it's not. We need a combination to open the door and we don't know it."

"X marks the spot, Momma."

"Try the year," Hana prompted.

Melanie put it in but they got a red light.

"The year the house was built."

Judging by what she'd been told by Luana earlier, Melanie tried that, still not getting in.

"Momma, X marks the spot."

"Birth years are as good as anything. May as well start with mine."

Once she had it tapped into the touchpad, the little red light came on again. Thérèse had watched closely, and then used her fingers to do calculations.

"You're old, Momma."

"Thank you, little girl. We'll have a talk about that later. Right now, we need to get this door open."

Thérèse sighed audibly. "I tol' you, X marks the spot."

"What do you mean?"

"Just like on treasure maps. They always have an X where the good stuff is."

"I still don't understand."

With another sigh, Thérèse tapped her fingertip several times on the touchpad. To Melanie's surprise, a tiny green light came on along with an audible clatter inside the door lock.

"See? Just make an X with the numbers. One, two, three, five, eight."

"That makes a T, not an X."

"Oh. It worked, right?"

Melanie grabbed the door handle and pulled. The heavy metal door came open with a creak. Opening it even more, she saw cobwebs stretch and break, and a musty breeze came up a set of stairs. The bottom of the stairs was in pitch black, but that wasn't their real problem right then.

Some chanting started in another part of the main house. Melanie recognized it right off as a haka dance being performed, and when the floorboards began to vibrate, she knew the heavy footsteps were closing in on her family.

It was exactly the same as when she was a child staying at the old bed and breakfast on that very same spot with her mother. A band of long-dead nightmarching warriors had come through the little house they were staying in, a moment of terror Melanie had never forgotten.

The terror wasn't because they were ghosts coming through in search of their souls. It was from the fact that the hukaiʻpo, or marching dead, could steal a mortal's soul if they were even looked upon by the living. As a child, Melanie hadn't known that, but instead stared them down as a stern warning to stay away. Now, she was hearing the same chanting as from decades before, and the same sense of terror flew through her mind all over again. Only this time, she knew better than to try and stand up to them.

"Kaimana?" Hana asked.

"I don't think so. It's more than one."

"Maybe he's brought friends to help us?"

"They're not mortal," was all Melanie could say. The door wrenched free from her grip and slammed shut behind her.

"Now what do we do?" Hana asked.

"Hurry. Get behind something," she told them.

Hana pushed the kids to behind the hanging hala mat, but it was too late. Into the spacious room came a foot-stomping band of Hawaiian warriors, dressed only in tapa loincloths and woven ti leaf garlands around their heads.

"Don't look at them!" Melanie said, trying to turn her family around. She clamped her hands over the kids' eyes.

Melanie knew they'd been found by the fierce ghosts and was already wondering if there was going to be another stand-off between her and them. Looking over her shoulder, she watched what was happening in the center of the room.

Continuing to stomp a loud haka dance, the ghosts assembled in tidy rows and columns, facing her. The last one to arrive was an old man dressed in the regal feathered cloak and headdress that had been on display earlier. He had a profoundly cross expression on his face as he glared at Melanie and the others behind her.

Wind blew with fury throughout the house now, whipping clothes and hair wildly. But the ali'i in front of her stood still as though he was unaffected by it. When he raised his fist that clenched a rock-headed mace, the haka dance ended. On the wind came the foul stench of rotting flesh, one Melanie had encountered before, and had never wanted to again.

"Who are you?" he bellowed.

"I'm…"

"She's my momma!" Thérèse shouted. Prying loose from her mother's hand, she took a step forward. "She's busy. You leave her alone!"

Melanie pulled her back by the shoulders. "Thanks Sweetie, but let me handle this."

"You're the mother of that clan?" the ali'i asked.

"Yes." Melanie had one card to play and had to play it right. There was more to this encounter than met the eyes, much more. Even though it had been over thirty years, she still remembered the fearsome face of the long-dead chief standing before her. She had faced him down as a child, and it looked as though she needed to again. "I've come to Molokai as ali'i of Maui, not for battle but in peace."

"You are an ali'i?" he asked, looking surprised.

"Of Maui. You don't remember me? We have met before."

He laughed. "And they are you warriors? Maybe that little one is your kahuna?"

"One of Maui's many kahuna. Be careful with her, for she knows powerful magic!"

At that point, Chance began to whimper, and Hana tried calming him. Melanie didn't dare look at Thérèse, afraid to see the expression on the face of her biggest ally right then. Melanie wasn't far from breaking down at meeting what she was certain were ghost warriors and their ali'i standing before her. She was equally certain they were nightmarchers, already out during the akua moon that would occur that night, the one night of each month they marched in search of souls.

The ali'i called for two of his warriors to come forward. When they stepped out from the others, they were even more gruesome, with hairy bodies and large single eyes in the center of their faces. Melanie had heard of these so-called 'akua' warriors, the fiercest of all Polynesian ghosts. While they slowly approached, Melanie whispered for Hana to tap the combination into the keypad.

Melanie could almost sense Chance shaking with fear, and Thérèse was beginning to whimper as the terrifying warriors approached, bringing the stink of ancient death with them. When she heard the door unlock and open, she turned for it.

Rushing, Hana fled through, pulling the wailing Chance with her. Just as Melanie aimed Thérèse for the doorway, a rock mace smashed into the door.

The metal door slammed shut, leaving mother and daughter on the outside of the panic room. It was Thérèse's turn to start crying, and Melanie wasn't far from it. She swung the girl around in a 180-degree turn, and headed off away from the two warriors. The girl wasn't moving fast enough, so Melanie swept her up and carried her along. Heavy footsteps followed their retreat.

"Magic, Tay! Do some magic and trip those guys!" she shouted, looking for a doorway.

"Momma, I…"

A spear flew past Melanie's head, just missing her, planting in the wall at the far end of the room.

"Just knock them down!"

No more spears flew, but there was a heavy tumbling sound. When she got to where the spear was anchored in the wall, she pried it loose and dared to look behind her. Both warriors were on the floor, their legs seemingly wound around each other, making them unable to get up again. Their aliʻi bellowed for two more warriors to chase after Melanie and Thérèse. By then, Melanie was already through a door, slamming it shut behind them.

They were outside, catching the brunt of the storm, the awning over the outdoor walkway flapping wildly in the wind. Still carrying Thérèse under one arm and the ghost's spear in her other hand, she ran the length of the exterior corridor and burst through a door and into a suite.

Inside, the room was calm, even as Melanie's nerves raged as much as the storm outside. She kept the spear in her hand.

"What the heck is going on?" Melanie muttered, setting her daughter down. She bent over, not knowing if she was going to get sick, or needed to pant for air.

"Those guys ghosts, Momma?"

"Sure were." Melanie did a quick inspection of her daughter. "Are you okay?"

"I okay." The girl winced. "Kinda worried about Brother and Hana."

"Yeah, me too. But they went into that panic room and the door closed, right? Is that what you saw?"

"I think so. Can I go potty?"

"Sure." When the girl trotted off to the bathroom, Melanie thought better of the idea. "Wait! Let me check in there first."

Once the bathroom checked out as being safe, Melanie closed and locked the door, staying in there with the girl, still keeping the spear in one hand.

"Those aren't happy ghosts, huh, Momma?"

"Sure aren't. Not tonight."

"Unhappy because the storm woke them up?"

"Unhappy because this is the akua moon and we're right where they want to be."

"Akua moon?"

They traded places so Melanie could go.

"Yes. It's the first night of the full moon. You know what that looks like. A big white circle, right?"

"No can see it tonight because of the storm," the girl said.

"But it's there and they can see it. That's the point."

"Cuz they're ghosts, right?"

"Right." Hoping her daughter wouldn't notice, Melanie blotted her eyes and blew her nose, trying to compose her nerves.

"Why can't we just ask them to go somewhere else? Maybe if we're really polite?"

"I wish we could, but I think those kinds of ghosts don't understand people being polite to them." Melanie took a slow deep breath and blew it out. She could tell her daughter wasn't keeping up with what was going on all around them. "Okay, story time. When I was a girl, my mother and I came to Molokai for a visit. Well, we stayed in an old house that used to be right here where this place is. There was a secret about that house, something my mother never knew I knew."

"Haunted scary place house?"

"Right. The lady that lived here was a ghost, and even the house was a ghost. Whenever we were in it, it was just like a real house. But when we left, the house disappeared."

"You guys weren't ghosts?" the girl asked.

"Nope. Real live people just like you and I are now. But that's not the only scary thing. That house was built right on top of an old City of Refuge."

"What's that?"

"The ancient Hawaiians had Cities of Refuge, places where people who got in trouble could go and live in safety and peace. In a way, it was like a prison. If they ever left it, they'd die. But if they stayed inside, they'd be left alone and could live in peace. Each island had a village like that. But the real problem was that they got nothing from all the other people on the island, and living there was very difficult. The place wasn't very good for growing things, and the one that was here was nowhere near the ocean, so they couldn't go fishing for food. Most of the people who lived in those places died terrible deaths anyway."

"And they became ghosts?"

"Well, if they did, they would've gone to Heaven as good ghosts. This big house was built right on top of that old village where people lived and died. I'm not sure, but I think those scary ghosts come here every akua moon to check on that old village."

"But it's not a village anymore, just a house," the girl said.

"But those ghosts can't see the house. They see the old village. To them, it's still a long time ago."

"This is a ghost house?" Thérèse asked.

"It sure seems like it. If I had known before we came that this place was right on top of that old village, I never would've brought you kids here. And I never noticed Halloween came on the akua moon."

"Pretty exciting Halloween, huh, Momma?"

Melanie blew her nose again. "A little too exciting for me."

"Me, too. Why for those mean ghosts coming here tonight?"

"Well, like I said, they march every akua moon, and that's tonight. They march because they are looking for something, or someone, maybe to finish an old battle, or a way to Heaven, I don't know what they want. But what I haven't told you is that I've seen them before."

"You seen these mean scary ghost guys with the big eyes before?"

"Yep, and they were just as scary then. It was when I was a girl, in that old house. They came marching right through walls and doors without opening them, like nothing was there. They looked so scary, and my mother was in another room. I didn't know what to do."

"What happened?"

"I stayed right where I was. I think I was playing with a toy, and I kept right on playing, but kept a close eye on those guys, by golly. Really gave them stink face."

The girl looked close to tears. "They come back looking for you tonight?"

"No. I think they're looking for something else, but we got in their way."

"Now we're stuck, huh?"

"Sure are. But somehow, we need to go find your brother and Hana and make sure they got into the panic room."

"You said the ghost guys can walk through walls, right?" Thérèse asked.

"Yes. So?"

"Why for lock the bathroom door if ghosts can walk through anyway?"

Melanie chuckled for the first time in hours. "Good question. That also makes me wonder if that metal safety door could keep them out of the panic room. I suppose not." She unlocked the door and readied to leave with her spear. "You stay here and keep the door locked anyway."

Thérèse bolted out the open door. "Forget it. I'm not staying here by myself!"

Chapter Four

As soon as Melanie and Thérèse left the bathroom, they stopped dead. Standing there as though they had been waiting were Kaimana and Luana. It wasn't so much they were in the room, but how they were dressed.

They weren't.

"Momma, they got no more clothes."

"I noticed that, Sweetie." Melanie pulled the girl back and put her hand over her eyes. She did her best to keep her own eyes trained on the young couple's faces. "I was looking for you guys a few minutes ago. I mean…"

"You left your room," Luana said. "I warned you to stay in your room tonight."

"Our room was demolished by the storm. We're lucky we made it to this one."

Thérèse tried pushing her mother's hand away from her eyes.

"Could you do me a favor and put something on?" Melanie pulled sheets from the bed and tossed them to the couple.

"Why did you leave your room?" Luana insisted, wrapping the sheet around her from the chest down.

"Yes, well, we got hungry and went to the kitchen. What's going on out there anyway?"

"Of anyone, you should know. The warriors are marching. Evil things happen when they march. You should have known that before coming here," Kaimana said. He wore his sheet like a skirt from his belly down.

"You shouldn't be here at all, but my husband insisted on allowing you to stay," Luana said, visibly upset. "He believes you can help with his fight against the marching dead."

"I don't care about anybody else's fight. I just need to find my son," Melanie said, going past them to the door, taking Thérèse with her by the hand.

"You won't survive if you go out there. Not even with that spear."

"My boy is out there! You think I'm not going after him?"

"He is safe, for now."

"Where is he?"

Kaimana answered in Hawaiian. "Ma hope o ka pale."

Exasperated, Melanie took a step toward the couple. "What's that mean?"

"Behind a protective veil. He is in the arms of safety."

"Yes, with the nanny. But she's no match for nightmarchers. I need to go find them!"

"We must explain…" Kaimana started, before he was interrupted by Luana.

"I'll explain. You don't understand about this place we're on. There was an ancient City of Refuge in this spot, a village of forsaken souls. Every akua moon, the warriors come to make sure the residents do not escape."

Melanie was close to hysterics. "I already know that! Just let me and my daughter spend the night behind that veil with the others until morning!"

"It's too late for that," Kaimana said. "You've already witnessed them during their march. You must help with fighting them."

"I'm not helping you or anyone else fight ghosts. We were trying to hide when they came. We want nothing to do with nightmarchers, ghosts, or the village that used to be here. Please believe me," Melanie begged.

"It is only on the first night of the full moon that the trapped and forsaken can escape. But Keanukakai, the ali'i of Molokai, and his warriors must not allow them to leave this place."

"And their souls are still trapped here?" Melanie asked.

"Yes. This village of refuge was built for only two very special people, and it is Keanukakai and his warriors' job to make sure they stay here forever more," Luana explained.

"But the kids, my nanny, we're all mortal. Why can they see us? Why should they want to harm us? We're not residents of that ancient village, and I certainly don't know how to fight ghosts."

"Once someone has been doomed to be here, they must never leave. But once a month, there is a battle for escape," Kaimana said. "And tonight, you've interrupted our ancient event. We've been waiting for endless moons for someone to come help. That must be you."

"Event?" Melanie glanced past the couple at the door again, still wanting to look for Chance and Hana. "What event?"

"My Luanapua and I are the ones trapped here for all eternity. We have been here for thousands of akua moons, and have never been able to leave this terrible place. We only want to go to Heaven."

"I'm very sorry, but why are we involved?" Melanie asked.

"Each akua moon, we try to escape this place," Luana said. "We have been trying for endless moons to leave, but we are always prevented. Each time, Kaimana must fight to the death, only to be reborn the next day. You and your family have gotten in the way of that."

"Luana suffers terribly at the hands of those beasts," Kaimana added. "Each morning after our great battle we wake, only to find ourselves still trapped here."

"So, you see? There will be a fierce battle here tonight. Your presence has already prevented us from possibly escaping, and will soon interrupt a great battle between Kaimana and Keanukakai's two fiercest warriors. Unless you agree to help us."

Melanie paced a lap around the room, thinking. "I'm very sorry, but I just don't care about the battles of ghosts, or whatever you are. I only want my boy. We'll be glad to leave as soon as the storm is done."

"I told you earlier, we need your help," Luana said. "Since the nightmarching warriors and their ali'i have seen you, you are now doomed to remain here, just like we are. The storm will wage for as long as you are here, and you will not leave until Kaimana wins his battle. You are cursed as much as we are."

"We're not staying! I'm sorry if I made a mistake in deciding to stay at this house this weekend. I should've gone to a resort like the others wanted. I'm sorry."

"You don't understand. You had no choice. We summoned you here."

"You what?" Melanie asked.

"We brought you here to help us. It's the only way for us to escape this place, to bring a mortal aliʻi here to help."

Melanie shook her head. "I'm only the mayor. I don't have any special powers. I barely have any power to make changes in our mortal realm. How could I possibly help you?"

"It won't be easy, but you're our only chance," Luana said. "Please help us."

"Momma, let's go get Brother and Hana and get outta this place. I don't like it here anymore."

"Either do I." Melanie stared at both Kaimana and Luana, trying to guess what was in their minds. But guessing what ghosts were thinking wasn't so easy. "It wasn't like this the last time I was here."

Both their eyes got big with disbelief. "You've been here before? To this exact place?"

"As a child. My mother and I stayed in Sandra's old house. It's a long story that I don't remember so well, but it must've been on the akua moon, because the nightmarchers came through one evening."

"You're the ones?" Kaimana asked, with greater disbelief.

"The ones what?"

"That escaped this terrible place!"

"I don't know about escape, but the next morning we packed out bags and left," Melanie said.

"But you were the one who saw the hua'kai po? You stood up to them?"

"Well, twice, I suppose. To your Molokai marchers, and to marchers on Maui. That was when I was carrying this little one," Melanie said, bringing Thérèse close to her again.

"You truly are the ali'i of your island!" Luana said. "You really do have the power to help us!"

"Right now, I don't care who is ali'i of anywhere. I just want my son!"

"If you help us, we will help you with your son."

"Help you with what? To leave here? I can't fight your battle for you, Kaimana. I'm mortal. I can't fight a ghost warrior. And I'm certainly not ready to become a ghost, just to fight someone else's ancient battle."

"You won't need to fight. You only need to provide me with a weapon that I have never used before."

"It's been many years since I was a warrior, and again, that was as a mortal," Melanie said. "I don't have weapons that could be useful to you."

"What is the greatest weapon a warrior can have?" he asked.

"Knowledge. Knowing how to defeat the opponent. With as little bloodshed as possible is best."

"Let me tell you a story," Kaimana said, finally sitting down. He waved for the others to sit, also.

"My husband's stories go on at some length," Luana said, again interrupting him. She took the spear from Melanie and leaned it in a corner of the room. "You see, we did nothing to deserve being trapped in this terrible place. It was all that Keanukakai's doing that put us here. Such a horrible, deceitful man."

As Luana told the tale of their lives, the story turned into a soap opera. Since apparently there was no way of finding her son unless she agreed to help them, Melanie did her best to remain patient and listen. "What happened?"

"We were still newlyweds, and Kaimana had insatiable urges as a husband. Somehow, that evil Keanukakai tricked him into visiting another woman."

Kaimana's head was hanging. "My Luanapua found us at the wrong moment."

"I don't understand how that got you sent to City of Refuge if you were the ali'i of Molokai?" Melanie asked.

"Keanukakai and his friend concocted a plan to kill the woman Kaimana was with, and made it look like I did it out of jealousy," Luana said. "When the elders met and discussed what should happen to me, they decided to have a special village of refuge set aside only for me and then put me there."

"Why is Kaimana here with you?"

"The fool decided to stand his ground. I guess he really did love me too much to let me go. So, he gave the ultimatum that if I were to be forsaken, he would accompany me."

"I was certain they would agree immediately. But those traitors turned on me and had me sent away also."

Melanie was confused. "But a City of Refuge was for people to live in until they died. After then, they would go to Heaven, just like anyone else, right?"

Kaimana's head sunk even lower.

"Except that Keanukakai convinced the village kahuna to place a curse on this village, and our souls, that we could never leave this place unless Kaimana defeated Keanukakai's greatest warriors in battle on the akua moon. Even after we died many years later and the flesh of our bodies had rotted to nothing, our souls have never been able to leave this terrible place."

"The kahuna hated you so much that he agreed to do that?"

"That kahuna was Kanela, the mother of Kahula, the murdered girl. Of course she agreed to put a curse on both of us," Kaimana said.

"It was only more trickery from Keanukakai," muttered Luana. "He tricked us all, even his own kahuna."

"And that's why you fight every month, to hopefully win the battle, break the curse, and go to Heaven. But I still don't see how I can help?" Melanie asked.

"We need a mortal to discover who killed Kahula, the wayward girl my husband visited one time too often, the daughter of the kahuna," Luana said.

Melanie continued to stroke Thérèse's back, who was now dozing quietly. "Why a mortal? You're ghosts."

"But we were all living when this happened."

"And you don't know who actually killed Kahula?"

Kaimana pled with his hands. "We do, and they do, but no one else. In order to remove the curse, the kahuna Kanela needs to know, and she would never take our word for it."

"It was all treated like a secret back then, something no one ever discussed, and the secret has followed us ever since," Luana said. "We need the secret to be known to history, exposed to a mortal for Kaimana to win his battle. That is the only weapon that he can use to win his battle."

Melanie sighed. "And since I've faced Keanukakai and his warriors before, he would listen to me?"

"By being a living ali'i of another island, you can help us. We tried to shield you and your family from this, but it's too late for that," Kaimana said. "Please help us."

Luana stepped forward. "You faced Keanukakai and his warriors before and didn't back down. You showed no fear. You are his equal, if only mortal. Being on the side of my husband in battle, Kaimana would have equal power to that of any warrior Keanukakai could ever bring forward."

"Doesn't mean I want to do it again." Melanie knew she wasn't gaining any ground with her refusals. "Look, I'm stuck in your nightmare with my kids and a close family friend. All we really want is to get out of this place, and if that means walking somewhere in this storm, so be it. At this point, I figure our chances for survival are better out there than trapped in here with a bunch of ghosts bent on revenge."

Kaimana looked up, now with a stern expression. "You're not getting your boy back until we're free of this place."

"So, you really are the ones that have them trapped somewhere? You're holding them hostage?"

"Yes."

"I know where they are, and how they got in." Melanie picked up the dozing Thérèse and left, cradling the girl against her chest.

"You won't find them!" Luana shouted. "There are dark places in this village you don't know about!"

As soon as Melanie left the room, she was blasted by wind and rain. Trying to see through the rain that was blowing sideways, she could tell there was more damage to the main structure than she realized. Much of the roof was gone, and many of the exterior walls had been blown out. Thérèse was just waking up when they got to an entrance door to the main building, and followed Melanie in, staying right behind her.

"No more ghosts, Momma?" she asked, clinging to Melanie's shorts and peeking around her hips.

"Still some ghosts, but we're looking for Chance and Hana. Where was that doorway? Do you remember?"

"Over there," the girl said, pointing a finger.

They hurried to the wall behind where the displays had been earlier in the day. Tossing aside tapa and woven mats, they searched in the dark for the doorway and touchpad lock.

75

"Where the heck is it?"

"It was right here, but no more," the girl muttered.

"The doorway is gone," Luana called out from across the room.

Melanie turned. "Bring it back to me! I want my son!"

"If you help Kaimana, we'll send you to your boy."

"Okay, I'll help. But promise me my son is okay!"

Luana walked to the middle of the room. While Melanie's clothes and hair were being whipped about wildly by the storm, Luana was completely unaffected by it. She laughed. "Or what will you do? Punish us more than we already are? Don't forget, you are a mere mortal playing a game in another realm! You are trapped here with us."

"You're not the only ghosts I know! And we have magic you have never witnessed!"

"What magic could a mortal have that is greater than ours?"

Melanie leaned down to talk to Thérèse. "Can you do your magic in a storm?"

"I think so."

"Can you pull her clothes off and throw them away?"

"I give it a try, Momma."

"Good. When I count to three. Ready?"

The girl nodded.

Melanie raised her arms as if preparing to lead a symphony orchestra and counted. Even she was shocked when the sheet that was wrapped around Luana unwound and flew away.

Luana retrieved the sheet and began wrapping in it again. "That was the wind. Nothing else."

"But the wind doesn't affect you in any other way. Admit that I have magic you can't control!" shouted Melanie.

"I don't believe you can call for a ghost!" shouted back Luana.

Melanie was far off into strange territory, and she knew it. With no other choice, she closed her eyes.

"Mom? Kinda need your help with something."

One of the sliding doors to the gardens blew out, flying off with the wind. Looking in that direction, she saw the silhouette of a figure slowly walking inside. The loose fabric of the shepherd's clothing was flapping around hunched shoulders. Using a cane as a guide, the crippled figure continued to walk in.

"Who are you?" demanded Luana.

The figure walked to the middle of the vast room.

"My name isn't important," an old man said with a weak voice.

"You're the ghost the woman has called for?"

"I have been sent here to help."

"A weak old man like you can help us?" Luana laughed when she looked at Melanie. "This is your magic? To bring this one to us?"

Thérèse tugged on Melanie's shirt. "Who that?"

"I'm not sure, but it might be your grandfather."

"Grandpa Jack or Grandpa Pops?"

"I hope Grandpa Jack."

"That guy the President guy? Your daddy?"

"I think so. Be quiet, please."

"Prove to me you're a ghost!" Luana called out.

The figure aimed his shepherd's crook at Luana. "Prove to me you're not mortal."

"I am the spirit of Luanapua, wife of the great Kaimanakeali'i, the one true ali'i of Molokai!"

Just then, there was the crash of lightning directly overhead. Terrible gusts of wind pulled away more of the building, leaving all of them exposed to the pounding storm. While Melanie and Thérèse were affected by the wind and rain, the ghosts were untouched by any of it.

"You've summoned me from my rest. What is it you want?" the old man asked Melanie.

"The Hawaiian spirits need a judge, a great ali'i in his own right, someone impartial, and someone who understands both the justices of the living and of the dead."

Just then, chanting in Hawaiian began somewhere in the distance.

Luana's face was illuminated by the flickering light of a kukui torch. "We have been cursed. My husband battles on every new moon, only to lose to trickery. For him to win the battle, we need to prove our innocence and to bring the real murderer of Kahula to justice. That is the only way to break the curse."

"You had your trial, but failed. Why involve these mortals in your spiritworld trouble?" the old man asked.

"Having a mortal ali'i witness is the only way to convince the ancient kahuna of our innocence," Luana said.

"And if I expose your criminal, you'll be satisfied?"

"Yes, of course."

"You'll reunite their family and leave them to their mortal realm?" the old man asked.

"Yes. You have my word."

He aimed his cane at Luana again. "Give them your word."

Luana looked at Melanie. "The ali'i from Maui has the word of the ali'i of Molokai."

"Where is the one who battles?" the old man asked.

"Preparing for his fight. Many prayers must be made. That is he who chants now. I am standing in for him now since we both suffer the same punishment."

"Bring me your suspects! And bring the accuser!" the old man said. He turned around and went to Melanie.

Melanie had to look closely at the man's face. Even though he was bent and crippled, he was still taller than her. "Dad?"

"Hi, sweetheart," the old man said weakly. Clinging to his cane, he crouched down to look at Thérèse. "Hello. Do you remember me?"

Thérèse scooted to behind her mother again.

"It's okay, Thérèse. He's your grandfather. He just looks different from when you've met him before. In fact, you might not even remember meeting him. He came to us one other time, but as a different kind of ghost than tonight."

The girl stuck out her hand to shake but remained behind her mother's hip. "Hello, Sir. Nice to meet you."

"You can give him a hug, but be careful. He's very old."

After the short embrace, the storm seemed to come back to them. Luana also called out she was ready with her first witness. A pair of warriors came in carrying the red kahili feather standards of the ali'i, followed by Keanukakai, and two more standard-bearers. They waited at one side of the room.

Melanie had to help her father stand up straight again. She and Thérèse watched as her father, Jack, a lawyer in the distant past, ambassador, and ex-President, walked to the center of the room. When he got there, he lifted his head and looked dead straight at the witness.

"Your name?" he asked the spirit of a beautiful young woman. Melanie could see why any young man would fall for her charms.

"Kahula. I am the one who was murdered."

"How did you die?"

"A curse was put upon me while I slept. I woke one morning to find I was dead. I've been this way ever since."

"You're not in Heaven?" he asked.

"I'm still climbing the tree to get there. So many branches, and it's easy to get lost."

"It was easy for you to get lost as a mortal too, yes?"

Kahula hung her head with shame. "Yes."

"You got lost and found yourself in a bed you didn't belong in, yes? That was the start of this trouble?"

"Yes. With Luanapua's husband."

"He is the great Kaimanakeali'i, chief of the island of Molokai! Say his name!" demanded Luana.

The old judge waved her to be quiet. "We all know his name. There is no point in wasting so much energy."

He looked at Kahula again. "Was it magic that killed you?"

"Yes."

"Kahuna magic?"

"Yes."

"The kahuna of your village?"

"One of them, yes. It was the magic of Kaleo."

"Are you sorry for what you did to Kaimanakeali'i?"

"To sleep with him after he was married to Luanapua? Of course! But I was tricked! It was Keanukakai that tricked me into Kaimana's bed!" she said, pointing at the ali'i who waited at the side of the room.

"If you had another chance, would you do things differently?" Jack asked.

Kahula looked confused by the simple question, as did Luana and Keanukakai for that matter. "With life?"

"Yes."

"I, well..." Kahula made eye contact with Luana. Both of their faces melted with sorrow. "...yes."

"Thank you. That's all I need from you," the judge said said.

Even though the wind continued to blow through the house, Melanie watched with pride as her father ruled the ad hoc hearing amongst several ghosts.

"Where do I go?" Kahula asked, still confused. The wind was now whipping at her simple clothing, the rain pelting down, soaking her.

"Away from here. Opportunities await you. Make good choices."

"Will I go to Heaven or be mortal to live again?"

"That's for you to discover."

Kahula left the large room, leaving through the only door that was still on its hinges. Melanie silently wished her well.

"Now, for the kahuna that cursed the girl into death."

A scrawny, bowlegged old man came forward. He looked almost comical in his ill-fitting loincloth, disheveled bone and shark tooth jewelry all over his body, and a wilted ti leaf garland on his head.

"You are Kaleo, the kahuna that cursed the girl named Kahula?"

"Yes, and let me say that I'm…"

"Quiet. It was a death curse?"

"Yes, and again, let me say…"

"Quiet. Who told you to put the curse on Kahula?" the judge asked.

The kahuna quickly glanced at Keanukakai standing not far away. "Who said someone told me to? Maybe it was my idea all along?"

"You're not wise enough to concoct a plan like that."

"What makes you think that?" the kahuna asked.

"If you were wise, you wouldn't have incriminated yourself with the murder of an innocent person, only to remain trapped in this realm and to wander this place forever as a nightmarching fool."

"Yes, well…"

"Did you concoct the plan on your own or not?"

"It was Keanukakai," the kahuna confessed after a moment. "May I go to my reward now?"

"This realm is done with you. I hope you enjoy what you find is waiting for you."

The kahuna nodded his thanks at the judge. Turning, he went to Keanukakai, doing his best to ignore the weapons his guards held in their tight grips. "Sorry, old friend. Looks like I made a mess of things for you."

"Shut up, you foolish old bag of bones."

Headed to the same door Kahula had used, Kaleo was stopped.

"That door is not for you," the judge called out. "Find another way."

The kahuna slunk off to an open door and went out into the storm. Melanie saw his body get caught by the wind and carried off into the night sky.

"Are you done?" Luana asked the judge, as Kaimana's chants became even louder. "What is your verdict?"

"There are more to hear from. Now, the accuser," the old judge said.

"Keanukakai!" Luana shouted.

Slowly, Keanukakai took his place in the middle of the room, still wearing his regal cloak of red and yellow feathers and his headdress. Two of his standard-bearers stood next to him. He stared sternly at the judge.

For the longest time, the judge looked back at Keanukakai without flinching. No questions were asked, no explanations given.

Finally, "You're guilty of murder and false witness against an ali'i."

"What? What sort of trial is this?"

"Better than the one you gave to Kaimanakeali'i. Guards, remove his cloak and headdress. Take those kahili away from near him. Luana, bring your husband. He is to be returned to his throne as ali'i of Molokai."

With a shriek of happiness, Luana rushed off to find her husband.

"I won't relinquish my throne!" shouted Keanukakai.

"It was never your throne to have," the judge said, still facing him.

Keanukakai pushed away the guards that were attempting to take his feathered cloak and headdress. "I will fight! I want to fight for the throne!"

"You have your chance!" Kaimana bellowed as he entered the large room. "But first, remove my cloak or I will take it off your dead body!"

"Wait," the judge said. "We have yet to hear from one last witness. Bring me the mother of Kahula."

A moment later, a crippled old woman limped to the middle of the room. Luana stood with her to keep her upright.

"Why have you brought me here?" the old woman asked. Her words came out as whispers.

"You are Kanela, the mother of the wayward girl?"

"Of Kahula, yes."

"You are a kahuna'ana'ana, the user of magic?"

The old woman coughed. "Yes."

"You're the one who cursed Kaimanakeali'i and Luanapua to this village of the doomed forever?" the judge asked.

"Yes." The frail old woman looked up into Luana's eyes and began to weep. "I'm sorry, Pua. You were like a daughter to me, as much as my own Kahula."

Luana kept her arms around Kanela. "We've always known that. You were tricked into believing Keanukakai's scheme, just like all the rest of us."

"The kahuna that tricked and cursed your daughter has been sent to his reward, and your daughter is now free. Does that satisfy you?" the judge asked.

She looked at Keanukakai. "I will be satisfied when the cloak is off that swine's shoulders."

"And then you'll remove the curse from this village of refuge? The forsaken will be able to leave?"

"Only after the ali'i's cloak is back to its rightful owner."

Luana helped the old woman off to one side to sit on the floor, and went back to face the judge. "Now what?"

"Now, the battle for ali'i of Molokai begins."

Chapter Five

The judge could no longer stand up straight. Back in his hunched way, he left the vast, empty room, going out into the storm the way he had come in.

"Thanks, Dad," Melanie whispered, watching him go.

The two gruesome one-eyed akua warriors stepped forward wearing hideous grimaces. Melanie couldn't shake the appearance of the single eye across their faces, deforming their heads. It was enough to make her want to run, but there was nowhere to go. Even though they focused their attention on Kaimana, Melanie pushed Thérèse behind her, wondering she was peeking from around her hip. When she felt her shirt stretch out, she knew her daughter was hiding her head beneath it.

Suddenly the storm outside stopped, right at the same moment Kaimana started a haka dance. As he chanted and stomped the floor, the two akua warriors did the same in return, the three of them facing each other. The more it want along, the louder and more powerful it got, and the more Melanie's leg was clung to by Thérèse. With a glance, Melanie could see the pride Keanukakai had in his ghostly warriors, smiling his satisfaction. After several minutes, all three combatants stopped as suddenly as they started.

One of the akua had a shark tooth club shaped like a paddle, while the other had a short spear with a stone tip.

Kaimana's hands were empty as his opponents circled around him.

"Always forgetting to bring a weapon to these fights, Kaimana. After so many years, you should know better," laughed Keanukakai. He tossed his own spear to Kaimana, one that was more ceremonial than useful as a weapon. "As always, I must help you in your sad effort to defeat my akua guards."

Kaimana didn't hesitate before thrusting the royal spear through the eye of a foe. With a second effort, he rammed it home, straight through the ghost's head and out the other end. Unable to pull the spear free, he left it in place and spun to face the remaining akua.

"Very good, Kaimana!" Keanukakai laughed again, but nervously. "You've at least killed one of them this time. But don't think I'm helping you again."

Kaimana and the remaining akua walked in a slow circle, facing each other. The akua took swipes at Kaimana's face with his shark tooth club, taunting him more than trying to inflict pain.

"You should've kept your spear, Keanukakai! I'm coming for you next!"

"You dare call my name, as though we're family? You speak to me with the respect an ali'i deserves!"

"If you were the true ali'i of this island, we wouldn't have been fighting all these years. I am the ali'i of this island and no one else!"

The akua warrior made the mistake of lunging too slowly at Kaimana, who simply blocked the shark-toothed club with his forearm and knocked him back. When the akua fell to the floor, Kaimana leapt onto him.

The club was swung, but too late. Kaimana got it in his hand and used it against his second opponent, ending the fight with one swing.

"Now, it's your turn, Keanukakai!" Kaimana said as he stood and turned. What he saw came as a surprise. A spear was waiting for him, the tip deathly close to his throat.

Keanukakai sneered. "Your blood will be on my hands this time, Kaimana, and it will be my pleasure to wear it with pride."

"You'd kill me in this way? A battle spear in your hands, and mine empty?"

"Your death is meaningless, no matter the manner!" Keanukakai's arm muscles flexed, ready to thrust the spear. "Time for you to rest until next akua moon, but not in peace!"

Kaimana stood straight and tall. "At least you'll be doing your own killing! Not like how you treated poor Kahula! You no longer have the kahuna or the akua beasts to do your dirty work for you."

"Prepare to suffer another moon, Kaimana!"

Before Keanukakai could send the spear through Kaimana's throat, there was a whistling in the air as the ceremonial spear flew across the room. As if striking an invisible partition, the spear stopped only inches from Keanukakai's eyeball.

"What...who threw that?" he asked with a broken voice.

"I did," Thérèse said, stepping out from behind her mother.

Melanie did her best to pull her back. "Not a good idea to get involved in their fight, Tay."

"My fight, too," the girl said, true anger in her voice.

"You're mortal! This isn't your battle!" Keanukakai complained.

The spear tip edged closer to his eyeball, the entire shaft wavering and shaking in mid-air. Seeing it hover like that, Melanie knelt down to her daughter's level.

"Maybe not a good time to use your magic."

There was pure anger on the girl's face. "I got this, Momma. Don't worry."

"What did I do to you?" griped Keanukakai, watching as the tip got close enough to settle on his eyelid.

Thérèse took another step forward. "You made my brother cry! And my momma is the mayor of this place, not you!"

"Mayor?"

"She is the living ali'i of three islands. That girl is her kahuna, and they have powerful magic," Luana said.

"That's the ali'i's spear pressing on your eye," Kaimana said to Keanukakai. "If that kills you, you would suffer the same curse as Luanapua and I have suffered for so long. Just a little further into your skull and you'd have no chance to ever go to Heaven, doomed to live in this village of the doomed forever."

"I know what it's for! No need to tell me about the ali'i's spear!"

"Remove the cloak and headdress and return them to their rightful owner," Luana said from where she stood in the corner.

"This royal cloak of feathers will never leave my body!"

"Until you are dead," Kaimana said. He grabbed hold of the spear and rammed it through Keanukakai's head, impaling the wall behind him. Keanukakai hung there like a raggedy old doll, now dead in every way, mortal and immortal.

Melanie watched as Luana went to the dead man and removed the cloak in silence. Shaking it once, she took it to Kaimana and draped it over his broad shoulders. After that, she took the headdress from Keanukakai's head and set it upon her husband's. Yanking the spear from Keanukakai's skull, he dropped to the floor. She cleaned the spear on one of the dead akua's tapa loincloth.

"Kaimanakeali'i, your royal house has been restored. Please take your spear and rule Molokai for all the future."

Melanie watched as they took each other's hands and walked away. As they departed, their bodies became thinner, transparent, slowly turning to mists. Getting to a wall, they passed through as though it wasn't there.

"Momma, where'd everybody go?"

Melanie looked at the floor where Thérèse was looking, the same place where the two akua warriors had fallen. They were no longer there, nor was Keanukakai's body. Even Kahula's elderly mother was gone.

Melanie got a shiver. "I don't know, but I think Kaimana and Luana have gone to Heaven together. That's good, right?"

"Yeah, good, but what about Brother and Hana?"

Melanie crouched down again. "First, I want to tell you how proud I am of you. You were very brave to do that."

"I got pretty good stink face, huh?"

Melanie chuckled. "You sure do!"

The girl winced. "Did I kill that chief guy?"

"No, not at all, Sweetie. I think you sure did scare him, though."

"That man and lady are okay now?"

"Kaimana did what he needed to do for him and his wife to go to Heaven. They've been waiting a very long time for that."

"I wasn't naughty playing with my magic?"

Melanie hugged her daughter. "You weren't naughty at all. But right now, we need to find your brother and Hana." They went to the wall where the doorway had been. It still wasn't there, not even the hole where the spear tip had struck. "I don't know how to get through the wall."

"Bust it!" Thérèse said.

"Maybe if it was a door, but this is a solid wall."

Thérèse left her mother for a moment. When she came back, she was dragging the rock-headed mace behind her. "Use this, Momma."

"Wow. Yeah, I guess if we're going to break through a wall, that would do the trick."

Melanie picked up the mace with both hands and swung it at the wall. It only bounced back at her, not even making a dent. Swinging a second and third time, she still wasn't successful at breaking through the wall.

"Let me, Momma," the girl said, grabbing the mace handle.

"It's awfully heavy. I doubt you can even lift it."

"I can't but my magic can."

"I'm not sure your magic will work with that club, Tay."

"You just said gotta use a trick to make the club work." The girl got her grips on the handle, holding it like a golf club, but looked up at Melanie for a moment. "Okay if I use my magic one more time?"

"If you can find Chance and Hana, please!"

Thérèse swung the mace as though it were a baseball bat as light as a feather duster, slamming it into the wall. What had looked like concrete only a moment earlier now tore like a papery mist. Once the cloud parted, Thérèse dropped the club and darted forward.

"Tay!" Melanie raced after her. "Wait!"

Instead of hurtling down steps, they were in a dark room, pitch back.

"Brother?" the girl whispered.

"Are they here?" Melanie asked. She waved her hands in the dark until she found Thérèse.

"Melanie?" a soft voice said in the dark.

"Hana?"

"I'm here!"

"I can't see you. Is Chance with you?"

"He's here. What's going on out there? Are the lights back on yet?"

Melanie stepped carefully in the direction of her nanny's voice. Groping in the pitch dark, she found Chance's slender body and took him into her arms. "I think the storm is over. Let's get out of here, wherever this is."

"It's just an empty room, but I couldn't find a way out after the door closed. I wasn't sure what to do. We'd just settled down on the floor when you came in."

With her free hand, Melanie felt the walls around the room for the door, but the mist had turned to solid wall again. Groping around, she searched for another door, a window, anything that might let them out. "Just settled down?"

"Yes. I felt the walls all the way around several times. After a couple of minutes, it seemed pointless, so Chance and I sat down and snuggled. That's when you guys came in. But where's the door you came through?"

"I don't know. I hope we're not trapped. How long do you think you've been in here?"

"I don't know. Maybe four or five minutes to the most. Why?"

Melanie wanted to laughed, but couldn't find the humor right then. "We've been out there for several hours, dealing with...never mind. Tay, where are you?"

"Right here."

Melanie sighed. "Where's here?"

"In the dark."

"Okay, fine. Do you have any ideas of how we can get out of here? Where the doorway might be?"

"It's a ghost room, full of weird kind stuff. Gotta think like a ghost to get out."

"Except we're not ghosts," Melanie said, still feeling the walls with her free hand. "But one of us knows magic, and that's weird kind stuff, right?"

"Magic?" Hana asked.

"You've never noticed that about Thérèse?"

"Momma?" Thérèse said.

"She tries to hide it, but I notice sometimes," Hana said. "It doesn't seem harmful. I never wanted to say anything, in case you didn't know about it."

"Momma?"

"It seems half of Hawaii knows Thérèse has magical abilities, whether we like it or not." Melanie banged her hand on the wall. "Right now, it would be nice if she could find a magical way out of this place."

"Momma?"

"What?" snapped Melanie.

"Sorry."

Melanie sighed again. "What is it, Sweetie?"

"I used magic to get in, right?"

"Yes, so?"

"I can use magic to get out again, right?"

"Yes. Do you know how?"

"No. Sorry, Momma."

"Back to square one," Melanie muttered.

"What's square one?" the girl asked.

"The starting point."

"Where we came in here?"

"I guess. I'm trying to think, Tay."

"Me too."

Melanie considered their problem of being trapped in a featureless, pitch-black room, without doors or windows, nothing at all to work with. Just like her daughter had said, it was a ghost room, full of kahuna magic that was working against them. Because Melanie rarely allowed Thérèse to use her magic, the girl had never developed her abilities with it. It was as though they had a key for a lock but no lock to put it in.

"Kaleo, that old kahuna, must've put one last curse on us before he left," Melanie mumbled in the dark.

"Momma?"

For some reason, Melanie wanted to change her name. "Yes?"

"I know how to get out."

Chapter Six

"How?" Melanie asked.

"No gotta use magic, either."

"Okay. How?"

"Gotta maginate."

"Got to do what?" Melanie asked. It was warm in the room and Chance was beginning to fall asleep sitting on her lap.

"Maginate. Like a story. We maginatered we got in here. Gotta maginate to get out."

"Oh. Use our imaginations. This might be a bigger problem than a bedtime story."

Thérèse sighed, a habit Melanie recognized as being picked up from her. "We maginatered the ghosts, right? We maginatered the big fight. We maginating being in this room. All we gotta do in maginate to somewhere else."

"She makes a good point, Melanie," Hana said. "I don't know what happened to you guys out there while Chance and I were in here, but it might be worth a try."

"Those walls felt awfully real," Melanie muttered.

"Trust me, Momma. I know magination stuff. All we gotta do is maginate to somewhere else. But we all gotta do it at the same time and to the same place."

"You're sure you're not trying magic?" Melanie asked. "That could really get us in big trouble if you get it wrong."

"Bigger trouble than we already got?" the girl asked.

"Another good point, Melanie," Hana said.

"Okay, fine. We're all going to think about going somewhere else. Where are we going?"

"I dunno."

"Just back to our suite," Hana offered. "Instead of sitting here on the floor, we'll all be sitting on the bed."

"Everything else is the same?" Melanie asked. "Same people, nobody added or missing, same time, spot, clothes, everything?"

"Too hard to do anything else," Thérèse said.

"What about Chance?" Melanie asked.

"He knows it. I already thinked it to him for to go where."

"If we ever get out of here and go home again, we need to work on your grammar, little girl," Melanie said, while tickling Chance awake.

"Huh?"

"Never mind. Mine's not much better. Is everybody ready to maginate back to our suite?"

"I'm ready," Hana said. "Mainly because I need the bathroom."

"Should we close our eyes to maginate, Tay?" Melanie asked.

"No need. Already dark in here. Can't see where we're going, anyway."

"Not very reassuring," Hana mumbled.

"Yay, you do the countdown," Melanie said. "And make sure Chance comes along, too."

"Countdown?"

Melanie sighed. "Everybody just start thinking about sitting on the bed together in the suite."

"What if…" Hana started.

"No what ifs. Just think."

For some reason, Melanie closed her eyes as she held Chance close to her. Having no idea of how long something like that should take, she spent several minutes of thinking about being on the bed in the suite. That turned into meditation, which almost turned into a nap. When her mind came back to the here and now after hearing an odd noise, she opened her eyes.

Chance had fallen asleep in her arms again, Thérèse was quietly snoring, and even Hana's breathing sounded like sleep. Unfortunately, they weren't on the bed but still in the dark room.

"Well, that didn't work," she mumbled.

She let the others sleep while she considered their situation of being trapped in the room. The misty doorway they'd passed through had closed as soon as they were through and couldn't be found again. There were no windows or doors, not even doorjambs that might indicate there could be a doorway leading somewhere. No seams in the walls or floor, just one solid structure in the shape of a box and they were inside of it. Fish in an aquarium. She'd felt every square inch several times with her hands. There was nothing.

Except…

"Wait a minute."

She laid Chance next to his sister and stood. Hearing the other three to continue to make the sounds of sleep, she set aside the fear they had travelled to the suite but she had been left behind for lack of imagination.

Following her idea, she went to a wall, extended her arms, and felt up to the top. Standing on her tiptoes, she stretched as far as her six-foot frame allowed. It was all blank wall for as far as she could reach.

"Rats."

"There're rats in here?" Hana asked, now awake. She made the sounds of hopping to her feet.

"No. I was hoping there might be a top edge to the wall. Or at least a ceiling. But there's nothing."

"What's that, Momma?" Thérèse asked, also now awake.

"Well, I was hoping there wouldn't be a ceiling. We never checked that. We only checked the walls and the floor."

"That's a good idea. Maybe you could boost me up and I could feel higher?" Hana offered.

"Worth a try."

Figuring the logistics of boosting someone in the pitch black, Melanie laced her fingers and got one of Hana's feet in her grip. After lifting a short ways, Hana told her to stop.

"Yes! There's a top edge!"

"Is there a ceiling?"

"No, just open air above the edge of the wall."

"How far up?" Melanie asked, setting the nanny down again.

"Just a little further up from where a ceiling would be. It's almost as if someone is trying to trick us, making it too hard to reach."

"If I boosted you more, could you climb over?"

"I'm sure I could. I could go first and wait for you to boost the kids over," Hana said.

"But how do I get out?" Melanie hopped a couple of times, trying to extend her reach. "I can't reach the top edge even with jumping."

"We might be able to find the door from the outside."

"That door is proving to be rather untrustworthy," Melanie muttered. She stood peering up into the dark, trying to see anything. "Who knows where you might end up even if I get you over the wall. It might not be in the same place as before."

"Gotta go potty, Momma."

"Me, too," said Hana.

"I think that's unanimous." Melanie felt Chance's small hand hold onto hers. It was the cool, clammy hand of a frightened little boy. "Okay, this is what we'll do. Hana will give me a boost over the wall and then I'll find a way to get you guys out."

"Momma…"

"You're sure you'll find a way?" Hana asked.

"Not sure of anything right now." She got into position to be boosted.

"Momma! Don't leave us!"

"It's okay, Tay. I'll be right back. You'll be safe in here with Hana."

"Momma, no!" was the last thing Melanie heard as she vaulted the top of the wall. Jumping down, she landed on her feet.

It was dark, nighttime dark, but at least there was ambient light. She was back in the same place, inside what had been the house. The storm was raging, and most of the house was in shambles, but the wall was there. It was solid, no doorway or entrance at all.

She pounded her fist on the wall. "Hana! Can you guys hear me? Bang on the wall if you can hear my voice!" She pounded her fist a few more times.

Listening with her ear against the wall, she heard nothing.

Melanie swore.

She saw the rock-headed mace on the floor a few feet away, right where Thérèse must've dropped it. Feeling desperate, she grabbed the handle and swung at the wall.

It only bounced back at her. With a few more swings, she was making herself tired faster than making a hole. Dropping the mace, she pounded her fist one last time.

She looked up to where the top of the wall should be. "I have to go back over."

Going several steps back, she made a running leap. Reaching as far as she could, there was no edge to grab, only solid wall. She tried again and again, never finding the top of the wall she had just vaulted moments before.

Stepping back, she gave the wall a solid kick.

"Now what? I'm stuck out here and they're in there. I'm really making a fool of myself, making things worse with my stupid ideas."

When she stepped back, she tripped over the rock-headed mace that Thérèse had used earlier. Lifting it to hip level, she closed her eyes and whispered a prayer. "I could really use some help."

Swinging the mace with all her might, it slammed into the wall and it bounced back. She let the mace fall to the floor again.

"Now what do I do?" she said, staring at the wall.

A hard gust of wind blew, throwing her forward. Instead of hitting the wall, she fell through vapor. Stumbling, she fell forward into the room, making a hard landing on her belly.

"Momma?"

Melanie reached out to find her kids. "Yeah, it's me. Were you expecting someone else?"

"Bring a ladder with you?" Hana asked with a sarcastic tone.

"No such luck. But I did go back to the same spot in the house. Most of the house is gone, and the storm is heavier than ever." She wiped rainwater from her face. "Did you guys hear me pounding on the wall?"

"Didn't hear nothing, Momma."

"You were gone so long," Hana said.

"Thought you went home without us," Thérèse said.

"So long? I was over there for only five minutes."

"Seemed like five hours. There's something screwy about time and this room."

"There's a lot screwy about this room."

"You couldn't find the doorway?" Hana asked.

"Just the wall. I tried jumping over but there's no top edge on the outside. I tried bashing through with the mace, but that didn't work either."

"How'd you get in here?" Hana asked.

"Not sure. I think I stumbled or something pushed me."

"Momma, I gotta go super potty."

"Me, too," Hana said.

"Give me a minute to think."

"No gotta minute," Thérèse said.

"Well, go in the corner, I guess. Just don't step in it later."

"You always say no make shi-shi except for in the potty."

Melanie's patience, and resolve, was being tested. "Well, we don't have one in here, Sweetie. We might have to break a rule."

"Not supposed to break Momma's rules."

"What do you suggest, that I toss you over the wall so you can find a bathroom?" Melanie asked.

"Might be able to kill two birds by throwing one stone," Hana said. "Didn't you say it was Thérèse who used the mace to break a hole in the wall, and that she used magic to do it?"

"Yes. So?"

"Let her go to the other side and use her magic with the mace again."

"You want me to toss my daughter over the wall into wherever she might go, alone?"

"I can do it, Momma."

"Melanie, you were just over there and said it was the same place," Hana insisted.

"With a raging storm, and a room full of trickery and a magic wall. And ghosts of Hawaiian warriors using spears and clubs to kill each other."

"Really gotta make super-duper potty, Momma."

Melanie found her daughter and held her by the shoulders. "Okay, you're going over. You know what to do when you get over there?"

"I know it."

"Tell me."

"Find the potty."

"But first, you need to break through the wall with that big club."

"Make a hole in the fog?"

"Right. And it's okay to use as much magic as you need to. But when you see the fog separate, don't come through. Just call to us so we know it's open."

"Okay."

"You understand, right?'

"I know it."

"But you understand that if you don't make the hole in the fog, we'll never see each other again?"

"Really gotta go potty bad, Momma."

"Okay. Put your foot in my hands and I'll lift you. When you find the top edge, just climb over and drop down. Just like jumping into the swimming pool feet first."

"Better hurry."

Melanie lifted the girl up until she felt the weight come off her hands. Soon, her feet were out altogether.

"Bye, Hana! Bye, Chance! Bye, Momma!"

Chapter Seven

"Where is she?" Melanie begged. A tear ran down her face while pacing another lap in the pitch-black room. "It's been hours."

"Maybe it hasn't," Hana said softly. "This room has been playing time tricks on us, along with everything else."

"I never should've let her go by herself. That was so stupid. I should've made her wet the floor in the corner like the rest of us have."

"You could send me over to look for her?" Hana offered.

"That's the tenth time you've offered, and no, I'm not sending anyone else into nowhere, or wherever she went."

"Do you want to go over?"

"Maybe I should. I can't just leave her over there. But I can't leave Chance."

"I'd be glad to go over…"

"She's been gone too long," Melanie said, interrupting. "Something's happened."

For the first time in the hours since vaulting her daughter over the wall, Melanie sat on the floor. It wasn't long before tears started again, even with Chance sitting in her lap.

Suddenly, the room got cool.

"Momma?"

"Thérèse! Where are you?"

"Out here. The foggy door is open."

A dull strand of light came from one direction, illuminating swirling mist. Melanie pushed Hana toward the sound of her daughter's voice. Following, she kept Chance right in front of her.

"Better hurry, Momma! The fog is going away!"

"Hurry, Melanie!" Hana shouted.

Melanie gave Chance a push. Just as he left her hands, the room got warm and dark again. She ran, but when she bounced off the wall, she knew she was trapped alone.

"Thérèse! Hana!" Melanie banged her hands on the wall. "Use the club!"

After too much time and too many tears passed, Melanie sat on the floor. The smell of what was in the corner was strong in the closed room, making it feel even warmer and stuffier. Wondering if she could somehow reach the top edge of the wall and pull herself up, she began jumping. For the longest time, she jumped and jumped, until she was too tired to continue. With one last attempt, she knew her reach was nowhere near the height she needed. She sat again.

"Mom? Are you around?"

"Why did you come back to this place?" her mother's voice asked.

"Mom! Are you…I don't understand. What place?"

"This is the same site as that bed and breakfast we stayed in a long time ago. You know that. You also should've known not to return."

"I don't care about that. The kids…Hana…I've lost them. I'm in trouble, Mom."

"I know what's going on. I've been watching the entire time, Honey."

"You have? Why haven't you done something to help?"

"I can't. Just like I can't do anything else to change the course of your life."

"Just tell me how to get out of this stupid room!"

"You have to figure that out on your own."

Melanie sighed. "Come on. I'm your daughter. You can't help me?"

"Yes, my daughter, and you have a daughter you need to help right now. But both of us are trapped in a circumstance we can't change."

"But you came here to be with me. You were able to change something that way."

"And you can be with them again, too. It just depends on what you're willing to do to make it happen."

"I'm all out of ideas," Melanie mumbled.

"Well, if you can't use your brain, use your brawn."

"I've tried jumping up to grab the top of the wall a thousand times, but I can't reach it."

"Three-hundred and twenty-six times. I counted."

"Not a good time to be picky, Mom."

"How many times have you tried going through the wall?"

"The wall is rock solid. It takes Thérèse using that mace and her magic to make a hole. I've swung that thing at the wall and can't even make a dent. It requires magic."

"Or faith."

"Yes, well, even with all the faith in the world, I don't have the mace."

Melanie waited for an answer, but it never came.

"Mom?"

Still nothing, only the empty feeling of being alone in a pitch black room.

"Yeah, thanks. Same old thing. Leave just before telling me what I need to know."

She rubbed her face, trying to get the cobwebs out of her mind.

"Just use faith as my magic?"

Melanie stood and went to where the wall was. Feeling it, she positioned herself about three feet back. Planting her feet, she balled one hand into a fist. Settling her mind, she swung with all her might, slamming her fist into the wall.

"Wrong kind of brawn," she said, trying to shake the pain from her hand. "Okay, forget brains and forget brawn. Just use faith."

Melanie stood with her feet apart, stared straight ahead, emptied her mind, and put her hands up. Stepping forward, she felt for the wall.

Feeling nothing on her hands, she took a step, followed by a second step. Still walking, she felt a cool mist on her face.

The vapor got light, illuminated by light from somewhere else. Focusing her sight and mind, she saw her arm lost in the mist, streams of light coming through.

"Momma!"

"There you are!" Hana said.

Someone grabbed Melanie's arm and pulled. She took several steps before she realized she was outside of the room and in the sunshine. Thérèse, Chance, and Hana were all there, smiling at her.

"Why for no come out with us, Momma?"

Melanie turned to look at the wall, once again intact, the mist gone. "I tried, but it closed up. Are you guys okay?" She went on an inspection tour of the kids.

"We're fine, but what about you? You must be starved."

"I hadn't noticed. How long was I in there alone? An hour or so?"

"We've been out here since yesterday."

"Yesterday?" For the first time, Melanie noticed it was daytime, and the storm had passed. The house was completely demolished, most of it blown away. Hana and the kids had a different set of clothes on than the last time Melanie had seen them. "What happened? Tay, why didn't you hit the wall with the club again to open the door for me?"

"Sorry, Momma. I kinda got tired."

Hana went to the girl's defense. "She must've swung that thing for hours. We decided to get something to eat, whatever was left in the kitchen that hadn't blown away. Then we came back and tried banging the club on the wall some more."

"No more good magic with the club," the girl said. "Sorry."

"That must've been why my mom came…"

"What about your mom?" Hana asked.

"Nothing. We're all out and together, and that's what matters."

"How'd you break the fog, Momma?" Thérèse asked when they went back to their suite to see what was left.

Melanie packed their few pieces of clothes that hadn't blown away into a bag. "With faith that I'd see you guys again."

"Faith is good magic?"

"Apparently so," Melanie said, taking her kids' hands into hers to lead them away. Surveying the carnage, palm fronds and debris was everywhere. She knew they had some walking to do before they got somewhere for a meal. But there was one thing she needed to do. "You guys wait here a second."

Melanie went back to the wall and put her hand on it. The door had returned, along with the combination touch pad. She tapped in the same numbers, and the door easily opened. Using a palm frond from the floor, she wedged it into the doorjamb to keep the heavy door open. Once she was satisfied the door would remain open for anyone that needed to use it, she joined her family again.

"I heard something about food. Let's find something to eat."

***

After finding a small diner in town, Hana got Thérèse cleaned up in the restroom, while Melanie tidied Chance, now wearing a tiny aloha shirt and shorts. With as smudged up as he was from enduring the storm all night, he looked much the part of a Hawaiian Tom

110

Sawyer. Melanie knew they still looked bedraggled sitting in their booth, looking at menus.

"Sorry we're so messy," she told the waitress. "We got caught out in the storm."

"You look like you were the storm. But that's okay."

"We do need a place to stay, or at least freshen up a little before going home. Know of any place?"

"I might. Let me make a phone call," the waitress said and left with their meal orders.

As if on cue, Melanie's phone rang with a call from her cousin David. Somehow, the battery had become charged again after the long night.

"Survive the storm?" he asked. "It made the news here in LA."

"Just barely. Do we have to talk right now? I'm still trying to decompress from a very long night."

"It won't take long," he said. "I had to send your resort ownership idea to our real estate law experts. It was getting too time consuming for me."

"You called me for that?" she asked.

"No. I heard from Josh's lawyer. They want to revise the settlement terms."

"Again?" She ground a knuckle into her cheek when her tic kicked in. "Now what are they asking for?"

"Josh wants the kids to come to Wyoming for Christmas break."

"I don't have the time off from work then. I've already agreed to cover for two other surgeons in the group. There's no way I can get time off anywhere near Christmas."

"He doesn't want you to come, just the kids," David said.

"What? Tell that…"

"Melanie, relax. His lawyer has assured me that if you agree to it this year, Josh will accept all the other terms in the settlement."

"And like I almost said a moment ago, tell that…"

"Think about it for a few days. Otherwise, you'll be hearing from commercial real estate about the resort."

The call ended quickly before Melanie could vent. She didn't get the phone put away before her next call came in. She didn't bother looking at the caller ID before answering.

"What?"

"Mayor Kato?"

"Oh, Chief Hernandez. Sorry. Just a little on edge this morning. What's new with the restaurant investigation?"

"First, did you get through the storm okay? They said on the news Molokai took a direct hit."

"We're fine, I think. Still a little frazzled to tell. What about the restaurant?"

"We've identified some latent prints from the scene. Before I tell you their names, I just want to verify that your restaurant was recently remodeled?"

"That's right. The entire place was gutted and completely rebuilt. And before you accuse any of the construction workers, I checked on the general contractor before the job and the company is solid. No complaints, no inspection red cards, no trouble at all. Completely licensed, insured, and bonded. But I seriously doubt any of their prints are still there, since the whole place gets thoroughly cleaned every day at the end of the shift. I stake the reputation of my family name on that place."

"It's been cleaned recently?"

"Chief, that place is as clean as the operating rooms at the hospital, you can count on that. At least when it still had stuff in it, anyway. Why do you ask?"

"That was exactly the answer I was looking for. One set of prints collected from inside the door, three different fingers, were positively identified. I'm a little afraid to tell you who, though."

"Not really in the mood for twenty-one questions, Chief."

"Your old friend Ozzy Simpson seems to have had something to do with the break-in and theft at the restaurant."

Melanie ground a knuckle into her cheek again. "So, he's back on Maui."

"Daddy's on Maui?" Thérèse asked.

Melanie put her finger to her lips to quiet the girl.

"It seems so," Chief Hernandez said. "We also found a partial match with another print to someone else, but we still need to investigate."

"Find Ozzy and I'll be a happy woman, Chief. Anything else?"

"Yeah. Are you voting for Detective Nakatani for mayor in a few days? Several candidates are waiting for your endorsement."

"Tell all of them not to hold their breath waiting for my endorsement. I'm writing in a name on the ballot."

When she hung up, she found three sets of eyes trained on her.

"Is Daddy on Maui?" Thérèse asked.

"No, he's still in Wyoming."

"What did David have to say?" Hana asked.

Melanie glanced at the kids before answering. "I'll tell you later."

"Momma, we're not having Trick'r Treat on Mol'kai tonight?" Thérèse asked.

"Didn't you get enough trickery last night?"

"I know I sure did," Hana said.

Thérèse slumped with disappointment. "I guess so. Never saw any other kids."

"Sorry, Sweetie, but I think we're all pretty tired and our weekend is done. It's time to go home."

The waitress returned with their meals. Seeing Thérèse starting to pout, she chuckled. "Well, good news. My mom runs a little hula studio with an extra room you could use for the day. It's right down the street. I know she has a room available. Her name is Kanela, and there's a sign out front for it. Just tell her Kahula sent you. That's me."

Upon hearing the name, Thérèse leaned into her mother for protection. "Momma, she a ghostie lady?" the girl whispered.

"I don't think so, Sweetie."

"Where did you guys stay last night that you're in such bad shape today?" the waitress asked.

"At the Hale Pakele. I guess I should go talk with the police about what happened in the storm. Somebody needs to know. Nobody else was around there today."

A Haunted Murder

"The Hale Pakele? On the edge of town?"

"That's right. Why?"

"I didn't know they rebuilt that place."

"Oh, you mean from Sandra's old bed and breakfast?" Melanie asked.

"I mean from the last time it blew away in a storm a few years ago. The last I heard, the owners in Honolulu had given up on building anything there."

"Momma…"

"Just a minute, Tay."

"Melanie, what's going on?" Hana asked.

"I don't know." She looked at the waitress again. "There's really no Hale Pakele? Because we got picked up at the airport by a van from the place. It even had the name on the side of it."

"Was the driver a big Hawaiian moke about my age, unruly hair, and kinda intense?" Kahula asked. She looked unhappy about something.

"That sounds like our driver, yes."

The waitress brought a chair over to sit with them. "His name was Kai. I was afraid he'd start showing up again."

"What do you mean, his name *was* Kai?"

"He was the shuttle van driver there before the place got demolished by a storm a few years ago. Actually, he perished in that storm. Every now and then, he comes back, if you know what I mean. He was such a good boy, everybody liked him. He was very attached to that place."

Melanie tried swallowing but her throat was dry. "Sounds like you knew him well?"

115

"We were lovers a long time ago, but he married someone else. His wife Pua worked at the Hale Pakele, and also perished in that terrible storm."

"Momma…"

"It's okay, Tay," Melanie said, trying to settle her daughter, even if her own nerves were starting to crack again. "By the way, what does pakele mean? It sounds very familiar but I just can't remember the meaning."

"Refuge."

■■■

Also from Kay Hadashi

The June Kato Intrigue Series
Kimono Suicide
Stalking Silk
Yakuza Lover
Deadly Contact
Orchids and Ice
Broken Protocol

The Island Breeze Series
Island Spirit
Honolulu Hostage
Maui Time
Big Island Business
Adrift
Molokai Madness
Ghost of a Chance

The Melanie Kato Adventure Series
Away
Faith
Risk
Quest
Mission
Secrets
Future
Kahuna
Directive
Nano

The Maui Mystery Series
A Wave of Murder
A Hole in One Murder
A Moonlit Murder
A Spa Full of Murder
A Down to Earth Murder
A Haunted Murder
A Plan for Murder
A Misfortunate Murder
A Quest for Murder

The Honolulu Thriller Series
Interisland Flight
Kama'aina Revenge
Tropical Escape
Waikiki Threat
Rainforest Rescue

CPSIA information can be obtained
at www.ICGtesting.com
Printed in the USA
LVHW111430141019
634125LV00005B/1882/P

9 781098 937515